ARI

Please note that this is a two-part series. This is part one, and part two is Memoirs of A Bad B*tch. Thank you.

BY TAUGJAYE

GIVE ME A PROJECT CHICK: ARI

2

TAUGJAYE

Copyright © 2020 TaugJaye
Published by Lucinda John Presents

All rights reserved. No part of this book may be reproduced in any form without written consent of the publisher, except brief quotes used in reviews.

This is a work of fiction. Any references or similarities to actual events, real people, living or dead, or to real locals are intended to give the novel a sense of reality. Any similarity in other names, characters, places, and incidents are entirely coincidental

GIVE ME A PROJECT CHICK: ARI

TAUGJAYE

DICTIONARY

The people from the city of St. Louis speak a language that was coined as *Country Grammar* by yours truly, Mr. Nelly, himself. To others, our Ebonics, slang, and diction is considered "Country." Throughout Ari's story, the use of this lingo is heavily embedded to give readers a little slice of our pie. The following words, phrases, and spellings below are provided to help you understand the language we speak, and to assure you that the book isn't riddled with typos, errors, and inconsistencies.

Li'l: The apostrophe before the "l" adds the emphasis we put on the word lil' in the hood

Chunk: Okay, alright; to make emphasis on a phrase or saying.

Bet: Same as the word Chunk, just a different phrase.

Words that end in "-ere", "-ear", and "-air" are typically pronounced with a hard drag of the word u. Examples are: Here and there. (Hur', thur') We also pronounce the words where, hair, wear, hear, and care like this too, but to keep the slang down to a minimal, those words are spelled correctly. Y'all know Chingy's song "Right Thur'."

Er'body/Ery'body aka everybody. These words will be used interchangeably, depending on context. If you remember J-Kwon's song "Tipsy" from the early 2000s, that's exactly how this phrase is pronounced.

"Bet you won't **swing on** him."
"She **swung on** her."
"She **stole off on** him."

5

"She *packed off* on her."
All of these are ways to say that someone threw a punch.

'Ery: Every.

Also, depending on the explanation, a word can or will be spelled with slang or correctly to fit the context.

Chinamen: Chinese Food.

Jammin'/Juggin': working hard, hustling.

Sumn'/Somethin': Something. These two will be used interchangeably. Same meaning, just different for context.

Nun': none.

I'on/You'on: I don't/You don't

Paypa': Paper, money.

'Er: Her.

Neva'/Eva': Never/Ever. Do you remember the song "Neva Eva" by Trillville?

Ia': I'll

Again, this story is about a St. Louis project chick and her hood, so the language is straight from the gutter, and I hope you enjoy it.

DEDICATION

To my big brothers Meechie and Scoo.

Thank you.

The days I sat up on the phone with y'all talking about the outline for this book are forever embedded into my mind.

ARI has done amazing. My readers love them *and* the impeccable way we carved perfection out of AB and Tress.

This story wouldn't be what it is without you two, and I thank you from the bottom of my heart.

Meechie.

My heart. My soul. I love you. Our bond is TO THE GRAVE. Yup, Big Meech, you've always had a play in my books, and saying I appreciate you doesn't seem like enough.

It'll never be lonely at the top, 'cuz bro, you, Lena, and the new baby are coming with me.

Lucinda John.

Thank you for believing in me. Thank your for that push, for the challenges, and for the way that you say NO lol. You have done amazing things for the ladies and I signed to LJP.

Love you, Lu.

They don't make 'em like you anymore.

-Love, Taug

GIVE ME A PROJECT CHICK: ARI

8

TAUGJAYE

1

"MAYBE I'M JUST A BAD GIRL,"

−DANITY KANE

FALL 2008

"Bitch, call him then! The fuck! I don't care about none of that shit you talking! Fuck you, and that bitch's broken jaw! I'll do it again after we come back from suspension! Think it's a game!"

"Ariana Kakos!"

"Bitch, I know my fuckin' name! You ain't my damn momma, Dr. Sully, so you can kick rocks wit' that shit! If you gon' call him, bitch, then call him!"

Defeated, her high school principal stormed out of the office. Steam was emitting from her ears like a raging train, ready for takeoff. Dr. Sully was so hot, her pale neck had flushed fire engine red along with her rosy cheeks and wrinkled forehead.

Ariana Kakos, aka Ari, had little to no respect for anybody. Especially her white ass principal who thought she ran Triple C Academy. It was her first year working for the chaotic neighborhood school. Ari would bet her last damn dolla' on it that the bitch wouldn't even make it through the winter break. Either somebody was gon' choke her tight, khakis pants wearing ass the fuck out, or she'd be pushed to quit from not being able to take the heat.

This was the twelfth fight she'd broken up this week alone, and it was only Wednesday. Yet, it was Ari's fourth brawl this school year, and it wasn't even cold outside yet.

Her knee couldn't quit shaking as she sat in her principal's office with salty tears streaming down her face. Her arms were crossed underneath her breasts. Her brand new, all-white, Air Force One's were scuffed and stained with splattered blood. All thanks to the bitch's mouth who she busted open 'cause she thought she could whoop her ass. A number of cuts were up and down her forearms, courtesy of that weak ass bitch getting her good with a box cutter. Her Aeropostale collar shirt was torn down the middle, exposing the polka-dot bra she wore. The once high bun that she rocked with her fresh micro braids was now a sloppy mess with patches decorating her edges.

Pissed wasn't even the fucking word.

Ari couldn't wait to catch that bitch on the block.

She'd break her other jaw with a sock stuffed with two locks or five dollas worth of quarters. With the way Ari was feeling, she was gon' knock *all* that bitch's teeth out her mouth, too.

This shit was not over.

Mark her words.

TAUGJAYE

Twenty minutes later, the scent of his *Curve* cologne caused her to roll her eyes so fucking hard, for a second, she thought they'd gotten stuck.

The look on his face matched the aggravation that was still etched across her own, but she didn't care.

Leroy wasn't even her real father. Her sperm donor was probably somewhere out in the KL, her hood, right this minute, penny pinching for another hit of crack. He'd walk right past her if he did see her. The only thing his bitch ass kept tabs on was wet pussy and getting high. In his eyes, he didn't have a daughter, and Ari could give a fuck about his dope fiend ass either.

"I just know you not on this bullshit again," Leroy spat.

He was mad as hell that Dr. Sully had interrupted his sleep. He should've been resting for the eighteen-hour drive he had to do that night out to Hampton, Virginia.

Leroy drove commercial vehicles for a living, but leave it up to Ari's smart-mouth and defiant ass, and he could never get the rest he needed. When he married her mother, Alivia, he never would've guessed that he'd have to put up with a moody and fast-ass teenaged girl. He didn't sign up for this shit, and with the way Ari had been acting an ass lately, she'd leave him with no choice but to put his foot down. Any day now, was bound to show this li'l girl a lot better than he could tell her.

"Nigga, bye. Just take me home. It's obvious that I'm suspended, so don't walk up in here on all that bullshit."

You would've thought it fazed her the way his jaw clenched and how the veins popped out of both his forearms and his forehead. The ones on his face shot up to his bald crown. Dr. Sully was scared than a muthafucka. She hid behind the tough exterior she'd built when Ari mugged that nigga up and down. She was afraid that he'd honestly slap the shit out of her from the rage that was brewing in his eyes, but Ari knew his Flo Rida looking ass wasn't gon' bust a damn grape.

That shit was all for show, with his weak ass.

"Ms. Kakos, it's a lot more serious than that this time around." Dr. Sully's voice cracked as she spoke, but she had to do her job. No matter how bad this seventeen-year-old, juvenile delinquent, continued to burn a hole through her chest with her evil glares. "This is your *fourth* fight this school year, and not to mention that you've assaulted another student with a weapon."

"*I* assaulted *her*?! That's some straight-up bullshit, famo! She swung on me, first! That bitch pulled out a blade on me! What the fuck else was I supposed to do?! How fucking stupid do you sound right now, bitch!"

"Sit yo' ass down!" Leroy threatened when Ari hopped up to her feet, ready to take her principle out.

Her mouth dropped when he had the muthafucking nerve to push her in the chest, making her ass kiss the seat again.

"Nigga, don't put yo' fucking hands on me! Is you crazy?!"

TAUGJAYE

"Ms. Kakos, ENOUGH! You're suspended for a maximum of ten days, and your hearing is scheduled for next Wednesday! You're only a few months away from turning eighteen, and the student's parents *can* press charges *and* try you as an adult. Her jaw is shattered from you hitting/beating her relentlessly with your lock, and you knocked three of her teeth out."

Everything around Ari froze. This bitch ass white lady was talking out the side of her neck.

She'd clearly just told her that it was self-defense, but no.

Her ass was grass.

She was the offender, and this was some straight-up bullshit.

The car ride home was quiet.

Leroy was so got damn pissed off, he couldn't help but clench the steering wheel with a death grip. He light up the last four of his KOOL squares, like a match, to keep himself from putting his hands on this little girl. It was enough raising her on his own. You'd think she'd cut him some slack after they lost her mother, but that was like saying water ain't wet.

"Don't slam my fuckin' door! Yo' ass don't pay for shit around this bitch, so you better act like you got some fuckin' sense, Ariana!"

"Get out my fuckin' room!"

She spun around on her heels, throwing her jewelry box at him in the same motion. Had his reflexes and agility not been A1 for his age, she would've creamed his ass dead in his shit.

"Leroy, didn't I say don't put yo' fuckin' hands on me?! Bitch ass dude, la'—"

"You'll what, bitch? HUH?!"

A smile swept across his face in a vexatious manner. He held the barrel of a .45 underneath her chin wit' her shirt balled up in his other hand.

Fear.

That was new.

He'd neva' seen not a lick of that shit form in her eyes until this very moment. Nigga felt so got damn tough and empowered, it almost got his dick hard to watch her unfold, just like that.

"What's that shit you was talking, Ari? Huh? Keep all that big shit poppin' like you was just doin' a li'l minute ago! Hot-shit ass girl can't say not a got damn thang now, huh?!"

He shoved her away from him with so much force that she fell back on her bed. It was inevitable to howl out in pain when she hit her eye on the corner of her nightstand.

"Fuck them tears! I'm sick of yo' ass! Unappreciative ass li'l wanch! If they put you outta school next week, then you gots to get the fuck up from out of here! I ain't dealing with this shit no mo'! You grown, then be grown, ho, but not up in my shit! You lucky I'm letting yo' ass stay here that much fuckin' longer! I can act a fool and put yo' ass out right now! I'mma be late to work fuckin' 'round wit' you! And don't yo' ho ass have no niggas up in my house or else I'll have somebody drag you up out this bitch!"

She jumped when he slammed the door behind himself. One hand was trying its best to stifle her cries while the other started to get saturated with the blood from her injury.

Ari picked up her mirror from off of her nightstand and screamed in rage at the sight before. She threw it at the wall, causing the glass to shatter all over her carpet floor.

Fuck that nigga.

If he wanted her out, then shit.

It is what it is.

By the time he'd make it back from his three-day road trip, she'd gladly be gone. He'd never have to see her ass again unless she came by and chilled on the block. She didn't need that nigga, and before she ended up in prison from murkin' his ass in his sleep, with his own damn gun, it was best that she removed herself from the equation.

Ari was in enough trouble with potentially being expelled—not only from Triple C, but from *every* high school in the state of Missouri. Murder was the last thing that she needed under her belt to top that shit off.

***

"Bitch, he did what?"

"Straight pulled a fuckin' gun out on me, Leah. When I say it's like that for his ass? I mean, I straight want that nigga head. Wait until I see what's about to happen with this hearing, then on my momma 'nem grave, I'm killing him. Bald head ass bitch got me fucked up—siiiiiii! Got-damn, Leah! That shit burn!"

"Then, bitch, quit moving. I'm tryna clean yo' eye so it won't get infected or turn into a sty. This shit is gross. It look like you got stabbed."

Ari looked into the mirror she was holding for the umpteenth time now. She shook her head while Leah put some more peroxide on a fresh cotton ball. People loved targeting her face because she was a pretty bitch, and they wanted to destroy her how ever they could. While she also knew that wasn't Leroy's aim, in her mind, he was still a hating ass nigga. His li'l stunt had just put him at the top of her shit list.

"Bitch, you got me looking like Nelly. What the fuck?"

Ari and her bestie shared a laugh as they looked into the mirror. A tiny band-aid was placed right next to the crease of her left eye. It was the first time she'd smiled all day.

"You still a ten though, boo. You hungry?"

"Damn right! And I wanna take a shower before yo' mama get off. That way, I won't have to leave yo' room. I'mma need a bucket, too, since the bathroom is right across from hers."

"I'mma bring Casey's li'l porta-potty in here. Bitch, that's the best I can do."

"Oooh, that shit is ghetto." Ari giggled.

TAUGJAYE

She gathered up her things for a shower while Leah went to whip them up somethin' to eat.

The hot water trickling down her back was just the relief she needed. She scrubbed her body with a pink mesh loofah, exfoliating with her favorite Olay body wash. She loved how the Shea Butter smelled against her skin.

A few tears were mixed in with the beads of water as she washed away the thick, Noxzema, facial cream. But the moment she stepped out, wrapped a towel around her frame, and wiped the fog from off the mirror to stare at her reflection, she swallowed the lump in her throat and held her head high.

Wasn't nobody about to see her sweat. No matter how many odds were stacked against her, and she was standing on that shit.

No, she didn't know what her next move was.

Yes, she was terrified about the hearing. Ari knew she'd already been skating on thin ice.

But, all she could focus on was today.

When she stuffed two of her American Eagle duffle bags with what all she could, and walked down the block to Leah's door, she was thankful when her best friend let her in without hesitating. Leah's momma was a cna and worked the evening shift. She slept all day while her little sister was at the daycare right up the street. The girls figured it would be easy dodging her for a few days. That gave Ari a li'l bit of time to think of a master plan.

Descending the steps in a white V-neck and a pair of pink booty shorts that her monstrous ass swallowed up, Ari smiled when she saw Casey. That was Leah's twenty-month old sister. She was crawling around the living room floor because her little chunky and lazy butt didn't like walking.

"Wassup, Fat Momma?! Look who's awake! Are you hungry?"

Casey's smile was adorable as Ari swooped her up in her arms and kissed her cheek.

"Grab her walker for me, boo, and bring it out on the porch with us. Let's see what's poppin' on the block. My momma just called and said she staying at work until 3 A.M. for some OT, so we good."

Minutes later, they were seated out on Leah's front porch in lawn chairs. The two were smashing some fried polish sausage on wheat bread with mustard, some plain Lays slathered in hot sauce, and some grape-flavored Kool-Aid.

The King Louis Apartments, known in St. Louis as the KL, stayed cracking. Ari lived, well, she *used* to live on 14th and Park. Leah stayed on 12th street. Her block didn't crack as hard as Ari's did, but shit, the hood was out tonight. There was a few more hours left before sunset, so that gave the niggas around enough time to get in one last football game on the street. After a certain hour, the dope fiends started popping out in surplus, searching for the dope boys to get a hit.

The niggas who didn't play ball were out too. They was posted up, smoking Reggie with their red bandanas in sight. Not to mention the matching t-shirts, caps, ball shorts, and anything else to represent the Blood territory that they lived on. The streets ran ruby red in downtown St. Louis. From the KL to The Projects, aka The Peabody, or "The Pissy Body" is what the Crips called them. It also extended down to the New Houses on 12th and Park.

Of all three sets, the KL came out on top.

It was a neighborhood filled with nothing but young niggas who were tryna earn their stripes. Off top, they stayed banging with them niggas from The Peabody to prove themselves.

Ari had been living in the neighborhood since she was in the second grade; these were her stomping grounds.

Niggas fought all day and so did the bitches. Only a few females in the hood were gang-banging and about that street life. When a fight broke out, it was mainly over money, dick, or somebody was talking heavy shit.

Ari was a pretty girl and that made her an easy target.

Standing five-foot-five in height with blemish-free, toffee-colored skin, she was as bad as they came. Built like a stallion with an ass so fat, that juicy thang jiggled with each step she took. Her Triple D breasts sat up so effortlessly, it looked as if she had them done. One hundred and forty-five pounds from the ground, she was stacked and solid in all of the right paces to only be seventeen.

Niggas in the KL posted up on the block at 3 P.M. faithfully to watch her and Leah walk home from school.

Her smile was radiant.

Her cheeks were a tad-bit chubby by nature, so when she smiled, her high cheekbones did nothing but enhance her beauty. You could get lost in her Whiskey-brown eyes due to her facial structure, and while most girls hated their noses during their teenaged years, it was her favorite feature.

You never caught her without her hair or nails done. A French-tip was her go-to style. She always got her name across both her middle fingers, letting niggas know Ari said, "FUCK YOU!"

If she wasn't rocking micros, two-strain twist, or box braids, then she stayed at the beauty supply. Purchasing a few packs of Milky Way to do up a new quick weave was like a weekly ritual to her.

It's how she kept money in her pockets.

Her bitch ass step-daddy barely wanted to feed her and keep groceries in the crib on most days. When she realized that bitches in the KL, and the other sets, were willing to pay her for a style that she could easily do in her sleep?

Oh, it was on and fucking poppin'.

Don't let it be a holiday. Her normal two-to-three hundred dollas a week would jump to almost a stack or more. Some weeks were lovely. Then there were times when she had to make fifty dollas stretch. Sumn' like a fat nigga tryna squeeze his ankles in some Air Jordan tube socks.

TAUGJAYE

Right now, she was down to her last hundred dollas. She couldn't go on a shopping spree or spend too much money on weed since she wasn't quite sure where the future was leading her.

Thank God she'd recently added French braiding underneath her belt. It came natural once she got the hang of mastering the use of her long nails and that kinky ass Kankelon hair. She could charge more and secure her bread on that note. With nowhere else left to turn, one thing she couldn't be was out here on some broke shit.

"Fuck you, Runo! You think yo' ass slick, fucking that fat ass, Baby D, looking ass bitch from The Peabody! I hope yo' money stay longer than that three-inch dick you got 'cuz I'm putting yo' ass on child support! I'm tired of yo' shit!"

Ari and Leah cracked up laughing at one of the jack boys, who often slid through to kick it with his peoples, going at it with his baby momma.

"Leah, never! Is that Queeny!" Ari gasped while holding her chest.

"Bitch, yeah, that's her. She know Runo will fuck anything walking as long as it got a pussy. Including hoes from that roach-infested Pissy Body. Ole' girl, Shayla, over on 13th street said he came over to fuck her the other day, and a dead roach fell out his dreds when he climbed on top of her to put it in."

"Put that on yo' momma!"

"Bitch, I put that on ery'thing I love!"

They broke out in laughter until the sound of glass shattering caught their attention. Queeny had thrown a brick when the car she was riding in had pulled off, busting out his front windshield.

Runo's potnas were in an uproar. They was laughing like fuck at what she'd done to his Impala. He, on the other hand, was hotter than fish grease in the middle of July.

"Yo'! Yo'! Ari-Ari, I got ya' juice."

She reverted her attention to Don, the local crackhead, as he approached her. He handed Leah the fruit punch Vess soda and Hot Cheetos she'd requested, then gave Ari the bottle of Melon MD 20/20 that she'd sip on all night.

"I know you ain't forget my damn rellos, nigga?" Ari smacked her lips wit' her hand out.

She impatiently wiggled her pretty fingers and rolling her eyes, waiting on her change.

Don was always tryna get over on somebody, wit' his junkie ass.

"Now you know good and damn well I don't want my ass beat. Damn right, I got 'em. I know you got them hands." He smiled with his one tooth poking out as he handed her the strawberry cigarillos. "I got me some squares too, so you ain't gotta pay me this time."

"I knew my shit was short. Hur', nigga. You lucky I fucks wit' 'chu."

He happily caught the ten-dollar bill she threw in his direction. His eyes lit the fuck up. The crack house would sure as hell be his next stop.

"Good looking, youngin'. I'll catch y'all later."

TAUGJAYE

Ari was too busy with the bottle up to her lips to respond to his funky ass. She wanted to run in the crib right quick, throw his ass a bar of soap, and tell him to wash underneath his fingernails. A dirty nigga made her skin crawl. To her dismay, there was no one else who'd hit up the corner store and buy her alcohol without questioning it, or wanting some ass in return, so shit. She kept his funky ass around.

Leah hated that her best friend drank at such a young age. Out of nowhere, ever since she turned seventeen, Ari would keep a MD 20/20, a wine cooler, or when she was desperate, a damn beer in close range. She was too cute for that shit, but the last thing Leah wanted to do was get on her girl's bad side. Especially once she'd gotten drunk, so she kept her mouth closed to avoid a collision.

"You scared?" Leah blurted out of nowhere.

The sun was going down now, and they were passing a blunt back and forth.

"Like fuck, but shit. It is what it is at this point. I hated school anyway."

"So, what you gon' do?"

"Like I fucking know," she expressed while blowing smoke between her plump, glossy lips.

"Pray."

"Nah, friend. I'm good. God don't fuck wit' people like me. If He did, then I wouldn't even be in this shit in the first place... *You* can pray for me though."

"'Ery damn day, boo. Trust and believe that shit."

"And that's why I fucks wit' 'chu, Leah. You a solid ass bitch."

"Oh my gawd! Ari! Thur' you go! I been walking around ery' where looking for you! Girl, I need my hair done!" This chick named Reesha interrupted them like she was in distress. She stayed over in the New Houses and had a shopping bag full of blonde and red wine Kankelon weave in her hand. "You do them long braids to the back with the curly ends and the pixie bangs, right?"

"Yop. A hunnid dollas."

"I got seventy-five now. My nigga gon' slide through lata' when he get off work wit' the rest. He should be here around 11:30. I want 'em all the down to my ass."

Ari knew Reesha was good for it. Her nigga sold Reggie over on the West where he was from, so she told her cool and stood up so she could sit in her chair. With Leah's momma working late, she had enough time to make some money. She'd be sure to break her girl off with some change for holding her down like she always did.

Maybe God *was* looking out for her in one light, but Ari wasn't gonna get her hopes up. She'd been dealt a shitty ass hand in life. There was no other choice but to deal with it as it continued to unfold. Maybe one day, things would start looking up for her.

TAUGJAYE

2

> "DEAR LORD, YOU DONE TOOK SO MANY OF MY PEOPLE,"
>
> –LIL WAYNE

If his damn phone was to ring one more fucking time in the middle of this li'l bitch topping him off, Audric would lose his fucking mind.

Some head in a comfortable bed.

That's all he wanted.

That's all he needed on a daily basis to keep his mind right, but every time he turned around, anotha' muthafucka was needing something. When he jumped into the game five years ago, he knew this shit would have him running like he was a quarterback in the Big League, but got damn.

Can't a nigga get some peace every now and then?

Niggas in St. Louis didn't sleep.

His pockets appreciated that shit. There was no doubt about that, but his mental was ye' close to being fried.

The more he expanded, the heavier his shoulders got, and the fuller his plate was served. That meant he had to hire yet another solider to hold shit down where he wasn't physically needed.

This had been a busy week for him. What he *should've* done was followed his first mind and caught that flight out to Miami. Three days of chillin' and fuckin' wit' a bad ass bitch on the beach sounded like heaven right now. But being the boss he was, he'd talked himself out of it since the blocks had been so hot. Damn, he wished he wouldn't had done that. The more shit kept poppin' off, the shorter his fuse got. In a minute, one of these nigga's momma's was about to be at the nearest Rainbow purchasing a new black dress. If his team couldn't get this shit under control, he'd have no choice but to resort to gunplay.

His patience was wearing so damn thin, his dick started going soft as he reached over for his pants. They were laying on the chair beside him, making it easy to search for which of his three phones was ringing.

Not the Razor.

Not the Sidekick.

It was his iPhone.

Shit was crucial.

Only a handful of people could reach him on this particular number, so when he saw the name 'Tress' across his screen, he didn't hesitate to answer.

"Yo'?"

"Get yo' ass down here on 12th and Park, nigga."

When his cousin hung up in his ear, that's all Audric needed to hear to know that blood had been shed.

His eyes flushed red as he grabbed the li'l bitch by the back of her head and pulled her from off of him. He didn't hesitate to start getting dressed.

"Damn, Audric. Why you always gotta be so fuckin' rough and shit when I'm the one pleasing *you*?"

His south side ho was always whining. Her cute li'l face was scrunched up. She tried to hide her attitude as she ran a wig brush through the bob that he'd fucked up.

One he wasn't paying to get fixed, either.

Ignoring her, Audric slid his feet inside of the navy blue Creative Recreation tennis shoes. He then snatched up his car keys, his Glock 30 with the extended clip, and dipped without saying two words to her ass.

His heart thumped against the bridge of his chest with rage. Triggered to the point of no return, he broke every traffic violation while floating his Cadillac CTS down S. Grand Blvd., racing for downtown. The hood could hear his tires screeching around the corner, way before they'd even caught sight of his headlights beaming through the dark and gloomy streets.

Audric was so heated, he pulled his car up on the curb and hopped out with an AR-15, M7, in hand while loading the clip.

His whole squad was out.

Everybody but his nigga, Dutch, and the thought made his stomach turn.

Tress shook his head when his older cousin walked up on him. All he could do was lead him behind the green door apartments to the back parking lot.

Audric's face was still, but he was trembling inside. He couldn't control himself when he made it around to the driver's side of the vehicle, and his cousin opened the door for him. Dutch's head was blown off. His blood and brains were splattered along the passenger's seat and the window. From the looks of his inside-out pockets, he'd been robbed, too.

A grunt from the pit of Audric's stomach transformed into a chilling roar when the sound projected through his lips. It took everything in him to hold his tears back. Never was he an emotional ass nigga, but Dutch was his boy.

He considered this man to be his family.

Dutch was his fucking brother.

They started this shit together.

They were the reason why niggas in the KL, The Projects, and the New Houses respected Crips.

Niggas 'round these ways wasn't dumb enough to step to them.

Not unless they wanted a shell to they dome.

Them weak ass snoops knew they couldn't fuck with Audric's and Dutch's clique, so to see his nigga murdered in cold blood, *and* on the grounds that they sold on, just ain't add up.

Shit was mad disrespectful yo'.

Somebody was dying tonight.

Audric wouldn't sleep until he made sure that he was the one pulling the trigger him damn self.

That was on his set. Straight up.

"That nigga Don said he found him like this. Say ain't nobody hear no gunshots either. The streets been quiet tonight, and you know don't nobody park back here like that, so *why* he was posted up is wild as fuck. Ain't no other niggas out here on no street shit besides us, so who the fuck else got a mu'fuckin' silencer to take him out? It's the only thing that makes sense when he'd just hit me up a hour ago sayin' he was headed this way."

Tress could hardly get the words out, the lump in his throat was so fucking thick.

The KL might've been wild in a handful of ways, but niggas knew to follow code. You see some shit going down that ain't have nothing to do wit' you, you turned the other cheek and minded yo' damn business.

Never step to a Crip unless you wanted yo' ass kilt.

That's law.

You see, the li'l niggas down these ways already knew Audric was a heavy hitta'. The Bloods didn't want smoke with hustling. Audric, Dutch, and Tress were the only ones jammin' in all three sets. Their rep was so official, *they* were the ones who migrated out north. *They* was the ones who brought out the hood, the guns, and drugs to Hazelwood, Florissant, Black Jack, and now, Jennings and Pawn Lawn counties, too.

Audric was eating.

He was gluttonous when it came to this shit.

The niggas in this hood were so out of touch with what they had smack dab in the middle of they own turf. He couldn't believe they was sleeping on the fact how the crack house was in the middle of 14th street.

Audric's and Tress' aunt lived on 14th.

Three houses away from the trap.

When they moved in with her, after both of their fathers were murdered six years ago, this set became their set.

Crackhead Don was the one who introduced Audric to the connect. He was already moving Reggie when they first moved in.

The money was cool.

Nothing to really brag about, but that white bitch sold like hotcakes at ya' nearest diner, and Audric wanted in on that shit. It ain't matter what it would cost him. The connect put him on because he respected his hustle—his brass demeanor and his hunger. Plus, he knew Audric's OG and was confident that he'd be on his shit.

It'd been nothing but cooking up work and having to re-up three and four times a week with the way Audric got to jammin'. When he touched his first mil in thirty days, nobody could stop him. He earned his success overnight, and it was only right to put his potna' on once he got his foot in the door. Then, his younger cousin, Tress, once he was a li'l older, and he'd started expanding.

His name was already hot in the streets because everyone knew he had them hands. He was from Baden down on North Broadway by the Ink Doctor tattoo shop. *That* alone told you what kind of man he was. He carried the heat on him now because he had to. The city of St. Louis was in the palms of his hands with moving dope. You could never be too cautious, but he didn't need a clip to prove himself.

He graduated from high school in 2003 from Gateway Institute of Technology. Aside from Roosevelt, Triple C, and Beaumont, the wildest neighborhood schools in town right now, Gateway was the hoodest magnet school around, and there was no room for bitch ass niggas in those halls.

Audric was fourteen when he earned his respect.

Freshmen Beatdown was a Gateway tradition, and the upperclassmen showed them li'l niggas no mercy. He might've stood six-foot-three in height by now, but back in those days, Audric was only five-nine, give or take a centimeter. This jock named Big Black was known for being the hardest and toughest nigga in school. That is, until he made the mistake for coming at Audric Bowden.

People called him AB unless you knew him personally or good enough to fuck wit' him on a first name basis.

Audric may have been on the shorter side back then, but he'd always been quick on his feet. He hit Big Black with that one-hitta' quitta', shattering the entire right side of his mouth. Dude needed it wired shut for a whole year. AB had that man talking like 50 Cent 'til this day, and everyone in town knew why.

Ever since then, he was respected by default, and him and Dutch were untouched. He earned his stripes at a young age. Audric grew addicted to the way it felt when niggas moved out his way whenever he came around.

He grew addicted to the way the upperclassmen watched his head and held his back like he ran the United States of America.

It's where he got his arrogance from.

His confidence.

So, when the connect, King Pharaoh, got word that Audric Bowden wanted in on his hustle, he knew he had the right man pushing his product.

Everything Pharaoh touched turned into gold. That's why people called him King. Until Audric started blowing up, you didn't see too many otha' niggas riding 'round in Caddys with thick ass, Mr. T, gold chains, crowding his neck and chest. AB wasn't nearly as flashy as King was. But he *did* stay rocking the hell out of a couple herringbone neckpieces to match his custom-made gold Rolex with the blue face.

He worked his ass off to get where he was today: a fucking millionaire at the age of twenty-three, and Dutch had been by his side since day one. So, to see him go out like this did something to his mu'fuckin' heart that he couldn't explain.

TAUGJAYE

The crew was quiet as they waited on a response out of their boss.

Audric tried his best to process this shit. His index finger and thumb dug into the creases of his eyes while he balanced the gun on his shoulder. Knocking on Momma Shirley's door at this time of night wasn't something that he planned on doing—*had ever* planned on doing, but...it all came with the game. Dutch's ole' lady was gon' be sick, and he knew it now that he'd be over there all night trying to calm her down.

"Get him outta hur', man. I can't stomach seeing him sitting hur' like this. Call the morgue, and somebody find that nigga, Don, ASAP. *Somebody* 'round this mu'fucka know sumn'. Tress, go up on 14th and see if Ms. Jenkins peeped something, wit' her nosy ass. Y'all go knock on these niggas' doors back hur', and don't fuckin' approach me until y'all got some info to run wit'."

***

Momma Shirley was in shambles.

She'd been hysterical since the moment Audric knocked on her door. All it took was that look in his eye for her to realize why he was standing on her front at close to one o'clock in the morning. The woman crumbled when she clutched her silk robe and dropped down to her knees, crying her eyes out. Audric's white tee was smeared in layers of mascara by the time her mourning had put her to sleep.

She'd been in a daze since, and he felt her pain.

Two solitary tears slid down his cheeks as he held an arm around Momma Shirley. She was a wreck crying on his chest while his nigga's casket was being lowered six-feet deep. It'd been a week since the murder, and Audric still couldn't put a face wit' the pussy who pulled the trigger.

Don swore up and down that he ain't know shit. Claimed the only reason why he approached Dutch's whip in the first place was because the shit was odd to see him parked in the back. He was just gon' spit a li'l something wit' his potna' and make a purchase. The chick he'd just fucked over in a nearby alley had gotten distracted. Another junkie showed up wanting his dick sucked, and he was able to pick her pockets. But when Dutch didn't roll the window down, like he usually would've done when Don approached him, he noticed something was off. Doin' the first thing that came to mind, he cautiously pulled on the handle, and found his body sitting at a quarter past fo', slumped over the armrest.

He'd never cross the niggas that supplied him with the best rocks he'd ever smoked. Getting in touch with somebody was his first and only thought.

Ms. Jenkins claimed she had just got home from a li'l get together wit' her peoples. She'd been chilling over on the Westside and told it like it was when Tress had questioned her. So for once, the neighborhood snoop ain't have shit vital to say.

The rest of the squad ain't have no luck either.

Shit was all bad.

TAUGJAYE

The simple thought had Audric grippin' the base of his clip that was tucked in the back of his slacks—he was so fuckin' disgruntled.

After making sure Momma Shirley was okay, he safely got her and Dutch's immediate family into a limousine.

Vanished was the sentimental aspects of his potna's death, and on came the heat. People could see the rage in Audric's eyes as he sauntered away from the crowd and headed towards his clique. They all were posted up by his ride.

"Aye, I got sumn'."

That was the best thing he'd heard all fuckin' week, but Audric prayed it was vital and not no he-say, she-say bullshit.

Tress waited on his cousin to respond. Yet, AB's silence, and the evident clenching of his jaw, was enough indication that he was impatiently waiting on the info.

"You know ole' girl, Leah? My homie that stay at 247 on 12th?"

"Yvette daughter?" He questioned while coolly rubbing his chin as his other hand rested in his pants pocket.

"Yeah, her."

Yeah, he knew her. Her momma could suck the skin off a dick, and she had some nice and tight pussy for her age. Audric may have bent her over a time or two on a coupla' her off days. She could cook, too.

"What about 'er?"

"Shorty just hit my line a coupla' minutes ago. She was cryin' and shit. Could hardly talk. Was scared to reach out and say sumn' to me until today."

"He was fuckin' her?"

"She eight weeks pregnant, fam."

Audric's chin fell to his chest while he shook his head.

"Said they been fuckin' for a while. You know Leah a senior wit' me, but she only sixteen. She skipped a grade. Her moms ain't too happy 'bout it. Shorty just found out she was pregnant a coupla' days ago when she took a test. Mind you, I had talked to Dutch a hour before Don even found him."

"So, he must've been laid up wit' her, then."

"On me. Shorty say he always parked in the back so nobody could peep how they was fuckin' around. Word is, he left around eleven. Said he told her he had to go make rounds and shit before he was due to meet up wit' me, but I called you at 11:30. Not even minutes after Don came and knocked on the door to tell me what was up."

Audric bit the inside of his cheek tryna play this shit out in his head. He was tryna imagine what the fuck could've possibly gone down.

"So, we got a good twenty/twenty-five minute window from the time he was still alive to when he was murked. She ain't see or hear nun'?"

Tress shook his head no.

"She went to sleep. Ain't even think nun' of it. Said he was usually in and out. Somebody was clockin' his moves, fam. Somebody know sumn' and ain't talkin'."

Audric ran both his hands down his waves, releasing a hard breath. Shit still wasn't adding up. I mean, it was *something*, but without a solid lead or a witness, they were still stuck in the same fuckin' predicament as before. He was really starting to lose his patience wit' this shit.

When he finally looked up from a moment of staring at his closed eyelids, the sight of a black, Pontiac Grand Prix with no plates and dark tents, alerted him. Creeping down the street, it forced AB to throw his arm around his li'l cousin and shield him while he removed an Uzi from his waistline.

A mixture of terrifying screams and blasting gunshots erupted in the air. Bodies were dropping; li'l kids were getting riddled wit' bullets.

Them niggas wearing ski masks and hangin' out the windows were bussin' for anything in motion.

On GP, Audric just let his finger squeeze the trigger. He was hiding behind the side of his truck with his arm over the hood for cover. Tires screeched at an uncontrollable rate when the unmarked car started to peel out. AB was now on foot. He held his Glock in one hand and the Uzi in the other, bussin' at them niggas back, hoping to pop a tire. The back window was all he could get, along with whoever was in the backseat on the passenger's side, thanks to the hollows in his Glock.

"Aye, Tress! Call Momma Shirley and tell them don't go to that fuckin' repass! Catch up wit' da' limo and take 'em to the safe spot!" he yelled before hoppin' in his holey ride and peeling out.

Fuck this shit.

These niggas took his potna out? Then had the muthafuckin' audacity to pull up at the burial? Like he was just gon' let that shit go?

Audric was hot.

Like a maniac, he floated his H2 throughout Calvary Cemetery, salvaging through the grass, running over graves, smashing headstones, and disrespecting hundreds of families' loved-ones.

He'd pay for the damages lata'.

These niggas wasn't getting away.

That was on Dutch's grave.

Floating on two tires, he swerved out of the cemetery ready for war. He was loading sumn' a li'l mo' heavy for times like this. Audric had 20/20 vision, so when he peeped the GT floating up W. Florissant, going towards the highway, he cranked his shit up. It was time to test the LH8 V8 engine in his shit.

Niggas already drove crazy as hell in the city. Adding him flying through red lights, switching in and out of lanes, and cutting people off didn't make it any better. His speedometer crept up on the hunnid mile-mark with little to no effort. It made the onlookers feel like they were in a *Fast & Furious* movie scene.

TAUGJAYE

His hand whipped the fuck out the wheel as he made a quick right, almost missing his chance to exit off on I-70 East. A li'l shitty ass Grand Prix couldn't shake his shit, and that was quite obvious now that he was on they ass. AB was thanking God like a muthafucka that he was left-handed right now.

Rolling the window down, he stuck his arm out. He only had six shots with the Smith & Wesson XVR 460 Magnum. This mu'fucka could take out a semi, but he had to be precise. His main thing was aiming for a tire, 'cuz above all, he needed a witness.

The way the horse-powered bullets lodged through his chamber, Audric could hear the sound crystal-clear over the engine roaring. The first two shots missed, but the next one popped a tire. The fourth flew underneath the back bumper, forcing the car to automatically catch on fire.

The Grand Prix started swerving out of control. It gave Audric the opportunity to pull up on the side so he could catch a face.

When he finally made eye contact with this nigga named Syd that knew from The Eastside, both confusion and rage filled him. AB blinked and his fifth a shell was in that nigga's dome. Just moments before the driver lost complete control and crashed into the median.

"FUCK!!!"

Four dead witnesses, one face, and now, he had to get the fuck out of dodge.

On top of getting rid of his favorite ride.

And even though he now had somewhat of a lead, it did nothing but raise further questions.

Who the fuck hired niggas from Illinois to hit up a burial?

Yet, most importantly, why was it a nigga that he'd put on and helped eat...before he was left with no other choice but to smoke 'em for dishonor?

TAUGJAYE

3

"IT FEELS LIKE THE WHOLE WORLD IS AGAINST ME,"

-LIL' WAYNE

TWO DAYS BEFORE THE BURIAL

Ari thought she'd feel some type of way when she heard the verdict about her being expelled. But all she could do was wear the same neutral and unbothered look on her face as she did then, while she caught the bus back to the KL, now. Leroy hardly said two words to her when she showed up for the hearing. She didn't have a cell phone at the moment, so it's not like he could call her. It's not like he'd gone out and looked for her either when he'd made it back in town.

Shit, that was one less thing he had to do.

He'd been making plans about turning her bedroom into a li'l at-home gym for weeks now. She did him a favor by speeding up the process.

The Big Red gum in her mouth was getting stale, but Ari was too stuck in this fixating daze to realize it or even care. Her mind was running a hunnid miles per hour, and it was making her eyes blurry. She wiped the tears that fell from her irises so damn fast that she scratched herself across the cheek.

Life had been nothin' but fucked-up ever since her momma was killed—one day before her seventeenth birthday.

She didn't deserve that bullet to her skull.

Nor, the one to her neck.

Or, the ones to her back.

It was the most fucked-up shit she'd ever had to witness. The thoughts would've sent a gut-wrenching scream through her lips. Had she not forced herself to eat the cries she so desperately wanted to let loose, shorty would've had a nervous break down.

Pulling the exit string, Ari didn't give a fuck where she was. She ran for the back of the bus and literally jumped off it, almost falling on her ass. Her anxiety had her all over the place. She hadn't made it far on her commute at all. It would probably take her a good hour to make it back to Leah's house from where she was, on foot, but fuck it. Ari pulled out the half-smoked blunt and fired up. The weed always helped her take her mind off the fact that her momma wasn't coming back.

She never fucked wit' Leroy. Ever since the day Alivia brought that nigga home when she was twelve, she despised his ass. She could see right through him like a broken blind in their hood. Only reason why his bum ass was workin' now is because he had to. When Alivia was alive, all he did was sit his funky ass down on the couch burning through squares, drinking up all the Kool-Aid, and eating up all the food. And he had her mama buying him weed every fucking day wit' her hard-earned cash.

Ari might've been young, but that shit was dumb in her head.

Her granny, Anne, taught her before she died, that a man was 'posed to take care of the house and his family. That nigga ain't do nun' of the shit her granny said.

He ain't give her momma no grocery money.

Pay no bills.

Nigga wouldn't even put gas in her momma car—the very car that he was still driving now, but was always gone in it.

Ari loved her momma to death. But as she got older, she still couldn't understand why she let that shit go down—let alone had married his wack ass.

Nigga wasn't even cute.

His muscles couldn't hide that receding hairline, or the fact that he looked like a mu'fuckin' mole rat whenever he ain't have on some sunglasses.

Leah always said her momma must've been getting fucked real good, and how he had to be eating her coochie just right.

The thought alone made Ari sick to her stomach. Shorty couldn't even think of her momma and Leroy like that.

She wouldn't know what sex felt like no way because she wasn't fuckin' yet and hadn't planned on doin' it no time soon. Niggas in the hood tried they best to get some of her kitty cat.

They would beg to eat it.

They would beg to fuck.

She could count on both hands and feet, and shit, even more, how many niggas in the KL alone tried to fuck her.

Some of they busted and broke asses was willing to rob they own damn mammies to pay her for a sample.

Ari couldn't see herself fuckin' nun' of them niggas, even if King Pharaoh himself tried.

It wasn't fuckin' happenin', but shit, that ain't stop the rumors 'bout her being a ho from going around. Leave it up to the bitches from the Peabody, Ari was fuckin' and suckin' er'body 'round them ways. Dusty asses only popped off wit' that shit 'cuz all they niggas wanted her. They was willing to pay for it before they even bought them bitches a Rally's burger.

Damn, it was hard being that bitch!

But, yeah.

Ari's momma was dumber than dumb fallin' in "love" wit' Leroy's punk ass.

She was surprised she almost lasted a year since the murder, living wit' him. Had he not started workin' and wasn't gone all the time, then he probably woulda' been and tried to put her out.

Ari was thinking so much that she made it back to Leah's house in no time.

The walk and fresh air did her some good.

The streets was quiet right now because er'body was still at school, so it wasn't shit goin' on for her to sit down and watch. Ms. Yvette was doin' a double, reason why her Trailblazer wasn't parked out front. Leah tried her best to get another key so Ari could get in and out. She claimed she'd "lost it," but Yvette wasn't having that shit. She told Leah to find the muthafucka or fuck around and be locked out the house 'til she got off at eleven. Shit, Casey had a daddy who could pick her up from daycare if need be. Leah was always losin' sumn', and Yvette was getting tired of her irresponsible ass daughter's bullshit. So when that plan didn't work, they started leaving the kitchen window unlocked for her girl to get in.

And yeah, they thought about Leah givin' her, her key since Ari would be there all day. Except, they didn't want nobody to see her goin' in and out the front once they really thought about it. Somebody would fuck around and tell her momma. They kept a guard on the backdoor when they was gon' 'cuz niggas 'round here will break in yo' shit and steal. Ari had no other choice but to use the window. It was a big risk to take, but Leah didn't care. Her friend was in need and she was gon' do whatever.

Some days Ari would do a few older chicks hair early in the A.M. and would leave wit' Leah when she went to school. Then she would sneak back in once Ms. Yvette burnt out for work. A few times, Ari had to hide in the closet whenever she didn't have nowhere to go that day.

Ms. Yvette never sat still. She was always walking around the house, and one day Ari had almost got caught. She had to think of some straight up crackhead shit and hide in a pile of Leah's dirty clothes one time. Ms. Yvette had came in her room lookin' for Casey's porta-potty. She was off for a change and didn't send Fat Momma to daycare.

Man, if she didn't have enough problems already!

Ari screamed like fuck when she climbed through the window and saw Leah walkin' into the kitchen. That was the last thing she expected to happen.

"Bitch, you scared the fuck outta me! Got damn!" Ari laughed as she popped the lock.

"My bad."

Leah's voice was low, as well as her eyes, and Ari could tell she'd been cryin'.

"Why you not at school, Le?"

"I came back once my mama left for work," she whispered.

"Bitch, what's wrong?!" Ari panicked.

"I'm fuckin' pregnant, man! Like, what the fuck?! Look at this shit! I can't stop fuckin' lookin' at it, Ari!"

"Preeeeeeegnant?!"

Leah threw the dolla test that she'd copped from the Salama Market up the street, on the floor, and cried her eyes out.

TAUGJAYE

Ari lunged for it, not giving a damn that her friend's piss was on it. Her eyes widened when she saw the two lines. Hell, she was cryin' too!

"Leeeeeaaaah! Oh my fuckin', gawd, best friend!"

She ran over to her bestie and wrapped her arms around her, huggin' her tight.

"My baby daddy ain't even alive no more, Ari! How I'mma raise a baby by myself? And that's if Yvette don't make me get an abortion!"

"Wait, bitch, what?!"

Leah stood up from hunchin' ova' and resting her head on Ari's shoulder. She then wiped her face and let her best friend in on the only secret that she'd ever kept from her.

"Me and that nigga Dutch been fuckin' for the last six months. I swear, Ari, I straight thought me and him was gon' get married. Like, I loved him. We been sneakin' around for hellas, and it's only 'cuz he was twenty-three. We both knew that shit was wrong, but it just happened. You know he be selling weed too. One day, I'm gettin' my momma some dime bags and he offered me to hit the blunt.

We sat in his ride, we talked, we laughed, and then, bitch, he had me on my back and took my damn virginity. Like, it came outta nowhere. He was so sweet to me, Ari. He made sure me and Casey was okay or that we ate. He would give me money, and all 'dat. It was weird as fuck at first knowing that I was wit' a grown ass man. Real shit, I was too embarrassed and afraid to tell you.

Like, when they found him dead, Ari, I just been fucked up. I was just wit' him. He was just hur' while you and Casey was sleepin'. Like, that shit gives me nightmares. And then, my period ain't came for a coupla' months and I been tryna keep my cool. That don't even matter though. I knew I was pregnant 'cuz we ain't neva used no condom. Best friend, what I'm gon' do? My momma gon' beat this baby outta me, and it's all I got left of him."

Leah was a mess. Dutch had her heart and she ain't been the same since he was laid to rest.

"Friend, you shoulda' told me! I neva' woulda' judged you! I ain't got no room to eva' do so, eitha'! I wouldn't fuckin' dare! You know I'm not that bitch! No wonder why you took his death so damn hard! Oh my gawd, best friend, I'm so sorry, baby!"

Leah cried the whole bus ride they took up to Planned Parenthood. Her ultrasound said she was eight weeks in. They gave her a whole bunch of pamphlets explaining her options. On the flip side, because she wasn't old enough, she couldn't get an abortion without parental consent. That ain't do shit but make her cry even harder.

Ari held onto her girl and let her cry on her shoulda' the whole ride back to the hood. She even kept an eye on Fat Momma while Leah tried to sleep it off, but when she woke up two hours lata', the nightmare wasn't over. The tears, and now the throwing up, was just startin' to kill her.

"Ain't no fuckin' way I'mma be able to hide this shit, Ari. I'm fucked," Leah cried.

TAUGJAYE

She pulled her head out of the new mop bucket that wreaked of her insides. Her throat was rawer than the chicken that her momma told her to take out for dinner.

For once in her life, Ari was quiet as fuck and ain't have shit to say. All she could do was hold the cherry flavored Blow Pop in the side of her mouth while she changed Fat Momma's diaper. Potty training wit' this li'l girl was not working out too good.

"Well, at least you not showin' right now. That gives us time to come up wit' sumn' until we can lay it on her."

Leah looked up at her best friend with a half-smile on her face. She appreciated Ari havin' her back through this shit despite what she was goin' thru'.

"So, what happened at the hearing? I ain't stopped not once to ask you 'bout you."

"Don't sweat it. They put me out of every high school in the state. Shit, fuck it. I'm almost eighteen anyway. Money can still be made without that stupid ass diploma. I ain't wanna go to college any damn way."

"Damn, girl. That's fucked up. How we manage to get ourselves into this shit? This straight cray-cray."

Ari put Fat Momma down and handed her, her sippy cup. It took her no time to clean up after changing her li'l chunky buddy.

"Crazy as fuck, bruh-bruh. But aye, we gon' get thru' this shit. I got you and you got me. You my bitch, and I ain't gon' leave you hangin', Leah, boo."

Leah stood to her feet and threw her arms around Ari's neck.

"Cheetah Girls for life, Aqua, boo," she joked while kissing Ari's cheek.

"Unnnn! Dirty! Talkin' some Cheetah Girls."

They busted out in laughter.

"Ho, that was you who kept hot sauce in yo' damn book bag for lunch period."

"Sho' in the fuck did. Them chicken sammiches was good as fuck wit' some Louisiana on 'em. You know yo' ass was right thur' wit' me and Tress bashin' 'em, too."

"Damn right! But, you know you can stay hur' wit' me as long as you need to. My momma stay pickin' up OT, and we been doin' good so far."

"Who the fuck is you to tell somebody that they can live in my damn house? Yo' ass 'bout to be out the door next, Leah."

Both girls jumped at the sound of Yvette's piercing voice as she stood in the doorway. She was dressed in a Tweety Bird scrub top and the matching pink pants.

Leah coulda' fell the fuck out at the sight of her momma once she built up the courage to turn around.

"Ma-ma!" *Casey cooed as she crawled over and tugged on her momma's pants leg.*

"You pregnant, Leah? I knew something was up wit' yo' ass, but I was tryna give you the benefit of the doubt. I was already gon' address Ari stayin' hur' once I got off tonight. After I found them clothes in the wash that wasn't mines or yours, I knew what was up. But fuck that right now. You think you fuckin' slick 'cuz Shawna called me as soon as y'all asses left Planned Parenthood. She was walkin' to the Aldi's and saw y'all walkin' in the door. Got me leavin' work all early and shit; fuckin' up my money 'cuz yo' ass wanna be fast. How far along is you? And who the fuckin' daddy?"

Leah was quiet as fuck. She couldn't even look her momma in the eye, let alone, find the voice to rat herself out.

"LEAH! I'M ALREADY SECONDS OFF BEATIN' YO' DAMN BACK IN, SO YOU BETTA' FUCKIN' ANSWER ME!" Yvette's voice was so frightening, it made Casey bust out in tears. She bent down and picked her baby up while patting her back. "Hush, Fat Momma," she said while kissing her chubby cheek. "Leah, I'm fuckin' waitin'. Got me scarin' my damn baby. If I put my hands on you, it ain't gon' be pretty. Now speak the fuck up, got damn it!"

"I'm eight weeks pregnant wit' Dutch's baby, momma!" Leah cried while droppin' down to her knees.

She was cryin' so bad, Ari got down there on the floor wit' her and rocked her friend back and forth.

The look on Yvette's face was fuckin' priceless. She couldn't believe this shit.

"DUTCH?! Leah...I just know you ain't sittin' hur' tellin' me that you was fuckin' that grown ass man?! And in my house?! What the—" She could hardly finish her sentence as she started pacing the floor.

Her sixteen-year-old daughter was fuckin'/havin' a dead, drug dealer's, baby.

She'd be the talk of the hood for months.

"That nigga leave you some money, Leah?" was Yvette's first question.

"He ain't know I was pregnant. I just found out today," her daughter sobbed.

Her momma threw her free hand up and scoffed in disappointment.

Just great.

Fuckin', great!

"Fuck it. I'm callin' that landlord back 'bout the house in Riverview that Lenny found. I was tryna let you finish school before we moved, but fuck that shit. We gettin' the fuck up out this hood. It's hard enough raisin' you and Casey. What the fuck we gon' do wit' anotha' mouth to feed, Leah? I make too much fo' stamps and yo' ass know that! You know what? You wanna be grown? You wanna lay up and fuck? Then you gon' take care of that li'l muthafucka yo' self!

I already got a damn baby! What the hell I'mma do wit' anotha' one? Yo' ass betta' get a li'l side job too! I'm barely makin' it wit' my income and child support put together, so as soon as you drop that li'l muthafucka, yo' ass betta' be the first one in line down at the welfare office! And call that nigga momma! I know he left her somethin' 'cuz, guess what?! She gon' help wit' this damn baby too!

Fuck that! At least it wasn't by no broke nigga, but still! And Ari, you can't stay hur'. I'm sorry, but we got enough goin' on, and I ain't gettin' in no shit wit' 'dat nigga Leroy ova' you. He already tryna sign his rights fo' you ova' to the state. Dat's jus' a rumor around the hood, but wit' you being hur' this long, it must be true. I'll let you stay the night, but I'm droppin' you off somewhere in the mornin'. This shit is too much!"

"Momma, she don't have no family. I'm all she got. Her granny dead, her daddy on dope, you know she just lost her momma, and won't nobody else take her in. Where she gon' go?"

Leah wasn't gon' let her girl go out like that. She'd beg her momma if she had to.

"Leah, shut up! Yo' ass barely got a fuckin' place to stay at this point! Matter fact, give 'er yo' bed then since you wanna be sista' save a ho!" Her daughter was quiet. "'Dat's what the fuck I thought!"

"Yo', you ain't gotta do me no favors, Yvette. I can leave right now," Ari spat while standing up to her feet.

Only reason why she was tryin' her best to remain calm was because it was her girl's momma, and she ain't wanna disrespect Leah. 'Cuz Yvette had Ari fucked up if she thought she was 'bout to be on this bullshit.

"Where you gon' sleep, Ari? Onna' corna' wit' the crackheads? Pipe 'dat shit down, you already hur'. But have yo' bags packed. 'Cuz after Leah go to school in the mornin', you goin' to the girl's home. I ain't catchin' no charges keepin' you from the state."

"The girl's home?! What the fu—hell I look like?!" She caught herself at the last minute.

"Like you ain't got no otha' fuckin' option! Y'all asses wanna be grown until it's time to be grown, then y'all wanna be some li'l girls. What? You was fuckin' 'dat nigga friend or sumn'? You can't go lay up wit' him?"

Yeah, Yvette threw a li'l hateration wit' that one. The image of Audric bending Ari ova', as he'd done her, was like a punch from Mayweather. She couldn't help it.

"Momma! She don't even know Audric like 'dat 'cept for seeing him 'round the block! Don't be like that!" Leah gasped while wiping the snot from her nose.

"Momma, nothin'! Y'all heard what the fuck I said, and 'dat's, 'dat! If you'on like it, then leave! End of fuckin' story!"

***

Ari could already tell that she wouldn't be here long.

Not long at fuckin' all.

The entire staff at the Covenant House women's shelter was fuckin' white. She saw a few sista's around, but it made no difference.

Ari wasn't even Catholic. She didn't claim a religion to be honest, but she knew God was real, and she did believe in a higher power. Leah tried to educate her on the Baptist religion and whatnot, but Ari had no desire to get into it right now. Maybe one day, but not today.

It was really bumming her out that Yvette was dead set on bringin' her to this bitch. It wasn't even a community center or even a fuckin' boarding house. It was an old school where the classrooms had been turned into rooms. The larger rooms could fit from ten-to-fifteen beds inside of them, and the smaller ones could fit one-to-thee beds depending on your luck.

She was thankful they had a space available wit' a smaller room versus a bigger one, so three of them now shared the space.

Ari grew up in the hood. It's not like she was scared or anything, but this shit was dirty!

Her mattress stunk, the sheets were dingy, one of them bitch's funky ass feet had the whole got damn room smelling like chili cheese Fritos, and she'd had a whole damn attitude after almost stepping on a dead roach.

It'd only been a full twenty-four hours that she'd been there, and Ari was already goin' nuts.

Most of the girls were Black.

Some was Mexican.

A few was white.

She shared a room wit' this Brittney Spears lookin' ass white girl wit' a fade and patchy skin, and she hadn't met the other chick yet. Word was, she worked hellas and was always in and out, but Ari wasn't checkin' fa' her ass.

Thank God she took a bath before Yvette dropped her off. She needed to hit up the nearest store and get a pair of flip-flops. Plus, some bleach before she stepped foot in the walk-in shower that was across the hall.

This place was makin' her damn skin crawl, her scalp itch, and all that shit. She wasn't feelin' this not one bit.

"Fuck it. I ain't sitting around hur' not a minute longer."

She couldn't stare at the clock on the wall for another second. They'd just been served Bologna and cheese, graham crackers, and apples for lunch, and her stomach was still growling.

After a quick ho-bath, she slid on a Hollister hoodie and some ripped jeans that she'd made herself, along with a pair of high-top forces. Her hair was now styled in twenty-inch, bushy/wet-n-wavy weave with a layered cut since it was parted down the side.

The wind had been blowin' hard against the windows in they room all day, so she knew it was a li'l on the chili side out.

"Ms. Kakos, don't forget that curfew is at 9 P.M., or you *will* be locked out all night," the old white lady sitting at the welcome desk reminded her.

"I know 'dat shit, lady. How many times is you gon' tell me? I ain't slow."

TAUGJAYE

Ari slammed the door behind her as she started to head for the nearest bus stop. First, she walked over to the closest place to eat which was a Church's Chicken by the intersection of Natural Bridge and Kingshighway. She grabbed her three chicken tenders, a chicken sammich, some fried okra, and a strawberry Fanta to fill her belly. Thirty minutes later, she hopped on the bus for her commute across town. She made it back to the KL just in time to stop at the Salama Market and get some snacks and some rellos. Since Don's li'l goofy lookin' ass was up there, he was able to cop her a MD 20/20 to sip on while she walked up to Triple C.

"Ayo'! What yo' ass doin'?!"

Ari jumped when she heard the voice screaming at her. When she recognized who it was, she calmed down. But then hurried up and closed the gas cap while throwin' the Snicker's wrapper on the ground.

"Shut the fuck up, Tress. Yo' ass gon' get me caught," she seethed while walkin' in his direction, away from the principal's car.

Tress shook his head, wearing a grin as he held his arm out for her. Instead of being given a hug, Ari punched his ass dead in the gut.

"Damn, what I do?" he frowned while holding his stomach.

"You a fake ass nigga. That's what you did," she growled while rollin' her eyes.

"You know it ain't like 'dat, Ari. Shit been wild since Dutch was murked. I barely been at school."

Ari wanted to continue on and throw a temper tantrum, but she knew he wasn't lyin'. The whole hood had been outta whack after hearin' he was popped. Plus, she knew Tress was out hur' tough in these streets, so she let his ass slide this time.

"Sorry."

Tress smiled before he pulled her in his arms and hugged her tight. Aside from Leah, he was all she had. Ari and Leah met in middle school, but she'd known Tress since elementary. He was the first friend she made when her momma first moved to the KL. They'd been dawgs since. Her heart only got soft for him, her girl, and Fat Momma.

It was fuck er'body else.

For real.

"Where Leah at?" Ari asked once they released.

"Her bird came and picked her up early 'round lunch hour. She called me while I was at the burial. And speakin' of that, that shit was wild as fuck. Somebody straight rolled up and aired it out on some drive-by shit."

"Are you fuckin' serious?!"

Tress shook his head, disgusted.

"Dead ass. Audric heated. I only came back for the last period 'cuz I had to take that stupid ass test, or else Ms. Langston was gon' be on some bullshit. I already got a F in the fuckin' class 'cuz I be skippin' so damn much. Leah tell you 'bout her and Dutch?"

"Yeah. We went up to the clinic the otha' day togetha'. Yvette went the fuck in on us. She lucky I ain't slap her ass in the mouth for poppin' off wit' all that hot shit. She was talkin' to me like she was crazy. I fights mommas too. The fuck?"

"Always tryna' fight somebody. Wild ass li'l girl," Tress joked as they started walkin' towards the hood.

"She was on some straight-up bullshit. Straight accused me of fuckin' yo' cousin and all 'dat."

Tress busted out in laughter, already knowin' why Yvette was on some salty shit wit' that one.

"What's so fuckin' funny?"

Ari cut her eyes at him. Waiting on an answer, she took a bite out of her Chico Stick before giving him the otha' half.

"Nun', man. How you holdin' up? When you due to come back? Bitches been walkin' 'round on some tuff' shit, already knowin' you gon' dead 'dat when you get back."

"They actin' tuff' 'cuz they know I got put out. I can't go to no high school in the State of Missouri."

Tress raised his brow.

"Damn, fa' real?"

"Yop. Whateva' tho'. I'm just tryna make it. Yvette dropped me off at a girl's home yesterday mornin'. Leroy put me out the day I got suspended, and I was stayin' with' Leah until we got caught."

"Hol' up, hol' up, hol' up." He ain't like what he was hearin' as they approached his crib. She was gon' have to finish explainin' this shit to him once they got settled in the house. "Aye, you gon' come wit' me while I get my pack, or you wanna chill in the crib for a few minutes?"

"Ia' come witchu'. King Pharaoh ain't gon' be on no bullshit, is he?"

"Nah, he know you my peoples and how I be lookin' out for you. I wouldn'a suggested it."

Ari held her nose once they were let inside of the crack house. It stunk so damn bad, she could've thrown up everything she ate that day.

"Sit right hur'. Ia' be right back."

He he handed her a 9mm to help calm her nerves.

It was shit everywhere.

The couch was filthy.

Ari sat on the edge of it for all of two seconds before coming to her senses. She realized that it was best to stand up while she waited.

It was empty baking soda boxes everywhere. Trash was all ova' the place. Half-naked big booty bitches were in and out the kitchen wit' scales, sandwich bags, and pots. Gucci Mane's "Mo Money" was blasting in the air. Fumes from the dope they was whippin' up kept seeping thru' the cracks of Ari's fingers that covered her nose.

This shit was crazy.

She was relieved when Tress finally came back down the steps, now wit' a Louis Vuitton duffle bag on his shoulder and someone wit' him.

TAUGJAYE

The look-out peeked out the curtain. He made sure the other look-out boy across the street motioned to him that it was all good for them to leave.

The hood wasn't too heavy wit' 5-0 patrolling they area. STLPD only came around when they was called. Profiling wasn't hot like that 'round hur', so it was easy to be in and out. Wit' all the li'l kids getting out of school 'round this time, the busier the block, the betta'. Er'thing they did was calculated.

King Pharaoh even had one of his super geeks, who was good wit' tech shit when she wasn't tweakin', set up cameras everywhere. They was on the block, at the front and back doors, and 'ery window on the second floor. He paid a nigga to monitor his spot 'round the clock. All the windows on the lower level had bars on 'em behind the curtains. They couldn't be seen from the outside. Plus, shootas stayed armed and ready in this bitch. He was always secure.

Five minutes lata', Ari was up in Tress' bedroom watching him bag his orders up. As always, she rolled her a fat ass blunt wit' his weed. He'd been smoking sumn' called Kush lately and had her tryin' it out.

"Now, what's this 'bout you at this girl's home and shit? I know I been busy, but damn. You been holdin' out on me, Ari."

She kicked her tennis shoes off before sitting up on her knees and said, "This shit been happenin' so got damn fast. Shit, I can hardly keep up. I'on know how long I'mma last at that bitch tho'. I got that feelin', Tress. That same feelin' from the night my momma got killed. The first bitch to pop off on me, I'm cutting her ass. After that ho Latifah caught me slippin' and cut me up when we was bangin' last week, I keep a blade on me now."

Ari inhaled from the blunt, feelin' it hit her system as she watched Tress. He divvied out the crack-rocks. He also got a book bag ready wit' hella 8-balls that needed to be dropped off in the county. They sold crack and cocaine.

Special order for a special customer.

"You a straight dope boy out hur', famo," Ari commented.

Tress chuckled.

"On me. I hate you goin' thru' this shit though, sus. Straight up. Hur'."

With the blunt secured between her fingers, she caught the metallic blue, Razor cell phone that he tossed to her.

"The number to my main line programmed in my Fav Five. Stay in contact wit' me, man. Fa' real."

"Tress, I can't pay no high ass T-Mobile bill. I'm still tryna stay on my feet. Wit' me all the way ova' on the Northside now, I can't get out here all the time like that. That bus ride long as fuck."

"I'mma keep payin' the bill, nigga. Calm yo' ass down." He laughed.

Yeah, Ari was all tough and shit, but she was a spoiled ass brat when she got around him. She knew Tress had her back. Plus, he was her big brother. And not on no, "we fuckin'" type shit eitha'. They were thick as thieves, no extra shit. Bitches wanted her to be a ho so bad.

TAUGJAYE

Er'body thought her and Tress was fuckin' too, but it simply wasn't like that.

Ari tried to hide how her eyes watered. She looked down at the phone in her hands *and* at the money he slid her—straight touched by his loyalty and concern. Shorty knew she could be free wit' him and Leah. Especially him 'cuz they'd known each otha' for so long. She could confide in Tress and not feel like a weak ass bitch for doin' so. But before she could tell her brother thank you, the door opened and in walked Mr. Audric Bowden.

He wore a scowl on his face, but that was normal. She'd always found it cute how his thick brows wrinkled, adding to his, how we St. Louis folks say it, schwag. He was shirtless with an upper body completely inked up in basement tattoos. They went all the way up to his neck.

P-R-A-D-A was across the band of his draws; they showed in the True Religion jeans that hung off his waist a li'l bit.

Gucci tennis were on his feet.

He smelled like Polo Black cologne, doin' sumn' strange to Ari's coochie. Baby girl ain't neva' felt no shit like that before.

His signature herringbone chains were around his neck to match his Rollie.

His hair cut was fresh.

Waves was bussin'.

He had juicy, Nelly lips, wit' some thick chin hair to match his neatly trimmed mustache.

And he had dimples.

Audric was on the slim side, only weighing in at one hundred and sixty pounds. According to the hood though, that nigga's dick was monstrous, *and* he knew how to fuck.

His skin was a russet brown color, he kept his fingernails clean, his eyes were brown, his teeth wasn't fucked up, even though he wore a solid gold grill on his bottom row. Ari couldn't tell for sure right now. Hopefully, she'd get some clarification on that one day. And last, but not least, his deep voice was just as sexy as it was chillin'.

Ari always thought he was fine but knew he was way outta' her league, so that's as far as those fantasies had ever got. Plus, he was always on the go, and she hardly eva' saw 'em.

Him and Tress slapped hands before he put six, thick ass stacks of money on the coffee table, and he left back out.

"You wanna ride around wit' me fa' a li'l minute? Ia' take you back out north wheneva' you ready to shake."

Ari nodded her head in agreement, now high as a damn kite while she passed him the blunt.

"Bet. Just let me finish baggin' this shit up, and we can shake. And if you need sumn', Ari, let me know. You know I got you."

TAUGJAYE

4

"IT'S LIKE I TAKE FIVE STEPS FORWARD, AND TEN STEPS BACK,"

−BONE THUGS N HARMONY

Ari was tired as hell. She'd been gone all day long doin' hair and managed to come up on a good three hunnid dollas. That was after doin' three girls in the KL some French braids just like the ones she did for Reesha last week. She almost missed curfew by being greedy, doin' Ms. Jenkins a French roll for fifty more dollas. Tress had got her there at 8:59, and the guard acted like he barely wanted to let her in—wit' his fat, chunky-neck ass.

All shorty wanted to do was shower and get some rest. She had anotha' long day tomorrow and wasn't lookin' forward to being on her feet for all them hours again. But shit, she needed the money.

Ari had to get her a spot, and her birthday would be here before she knew it. She had a good five weeks until she hit the big one-eight, and she wanted the money in hand to match Tress for her move-in dues. Plus, she was gon' need food, house supplies, and a damn bed.

She wasn't sleepin' on no damn flo'.

Hell no.

Tress refused to give her the whole thing. Her brother was teaching her the code of hustle and letting her see how vital it was to stay on her shit. Wasn't nobody out here in this world gon' give you shit, and ain't a soul alive owe you shit either. Only the people who brought you into this world did, and since that was all bad for Ari, she had to step up at a early age and look out for herself.

Hustlin' for bread wasn't new to her, but now she had to go hard on the paint wit' that shit. This was more than just keepin' money in her pockets for food, clothes, and leisure means. She was on some survival shit now that she was technically on her own.

Tress planned on givin' Ari the money back once she got all moved in, but she ain't know that. He was pushing her and wanted her to remain focused on something positive. It was way too easy to get sucked up in chillin' on the block, blowin' yo' money on stupid shit, and clubbin'. She was too headstrong for that. Tress wasn't gon' let that girl lose herself, so he kept her busy by givin' her a goal to reach.

Ari's mind wasn't right, right now. She was still hurtin' ova' her moms, and that anniversary was approachin' quickly. Knowing it was coming, it made her attitude shittier than usual. Leroy was walkin' around actin' a ass now since her papers was pending wit' the state. And since her mama was dead, Ari technically wasn't his responsibility. He was fightin' hard for that shit, wit' his bitch ass.

Tress knew she was goin' thru' it, but sittin' around all lost and depressed wasn't gon' solve the problem. He knew what it was like to lose a parent. Shit, boffum. He felt her on that a hunnid percent, but life still goes on. Besides Leah, he was the only person Ari listened to, so he was hard on her because she needed that guidance no matter what she said. She could cuss his ass out all day long if she wanted to. It didn't faze Tress. He could really give a fuck about her givin' him no lip. That ass was workin' for that paypa' and sumn' better, wasn't she?

And that's all that mattered.

After her shower, Ari decided to go down to the TV room and watch a movie. All of a sudden, she wasn't that sleepy but didn't want to stare at the walls and possibly find anotha' thing about this stupid ass place that would piss her off. This had been the longest fuckin' week of her damn life being up in this bitch.

Wit' a bag of Flammin' Hot Cheetos and a Strawberry-Melon Brisk juice in hand, she took the steps down to the first floor. She shoulda' known it was gon' be packed since it was Friday night. All eyes was on her when she walked over to a empty recliner and took a seat. Bitches was straight muggin', and for once in her life, Ari wasn't even on no otha' shit. She was just tryna chill, but the pointin' and glarin' and turnt up noses just wouldn't quit, and now she was all the way triggered.

"The fuck? Y'all bitches got a problem or sumn'? Y'all speak English just like I do, so eitha' step, or shut the fuck up!" Ari yelled while hoppin' up to her feet, knocking her chips on the floor when she did so.

With that, the so-called "ringleader" stood up too while pullin' her hair back. That forced Ari to do the same wit' the rubber band she had around her wrist.

Fuck, I forgot my damn blade!

Oh well. She was still lethal wit' out it. Shit, she'd take all these bitches if she had to. Like Da Bangas said, *"Ain't no bitch in me, nigga!"*

The light-skinned girl then unzipped her jacket after she secured her ponytail and handed it to one of her homegirls while she laughed out loud.

"Latifah my mu'fuckin' li'l cousin, bitch. She been eating out a straw for weeks 'cuz yo' pussy ass wanna be a ho and fuck anotha' bitch's man. Then, you can't use yo' hands or settle for gettin' yo' ass beat. I'm 'bout to rock yo' shit like you did hers. Look at God sending you right to yo' maker ho—"

"Damn!"

Ari's eyes flushed red when she picked up the metal folding chair that was near her and swung it at that bitch. Teeth flew out ole' girl's mouth before Ari lunged at her, tackled her, and then started throwin' mean ass blows to her face.

She had a short fuse.

Mu'fuckas new that, yet it was obvious that this ho didn't. It was only right to show her a lot betta' than she could tell her.

Ari was whoopin' ass with blood splattering everywhere. It didn't surprise her when anotha' girl jumped in. The chick grabbed her by her weave and pulled her off of Latifah's cousin. Another girl tried to jump in and get on top of Ari, but she was quick and kicked that bitch dead in her face on some KO shit. Ari then scrambled back up to her feet and might've got her lip busted in the process, but once she got a good grip on the bitch's hair, the punches came so hard, she heard the girl's nose crack. She then grabbed this ho by the shirt and threw her ass into the TV that was sitting inside of an entertainment center, knocking movies over and splitting the wood.

The loud sound of a whistle blowing in the air snapped Ari out of her rage. It made her notice when the security guard barged in the room and ran towards her. She started swinging on his ass too, but she was no match for the fat fuck. He body-slammed her so hard onto the floor that it had her seeing stars for a li'l minute. When they cleared, she started back fighting at his ass again.

"Get yo' fat ass off me! She shouldn't a been talkin' shit! I said get yo' damn hands off me, you bitch ass nigga!"

"ARIANA KAKOS!" the warden over the building yelled in panic.

When she ran in the room and saw the aftermath from Ari's outburst, her blood pressure skyrocketed.

"It ain't my fault! I was mindin' my own fuckin' business, and she stepped to me! I told y'all bitches I didn't play that shit! Now yo' ass can eat out a fuckin' straw right along wit' yo' ho ass cousin, bitch!"

"Take her to my office and get a nurse in here!" the frightened warden cried.

She helped one of the three girls, who were severely injured up, to her feet.

Ari was so got damn mad that she flipped the warden's desk over after the security officer locked her inside of her room. Bitches was always coming for her. Ari ain't even have beef wit' Latifah. Latifah assumed that she was fuckin' her man because of some he-say, she-say, and she ran wit' it.

Ari was minding her business like she always did that day. She was tryna put her shit in her locker so she could meet up wit' Tress for lunch. Leah was out on a field trip, so it was just gon' be them two that time around. By the time she had her lock unlocked, Ari caught Latifah out the side of her eye swingin' on her. Like the project chick she was, she started swingin' on her ass back!

Now she was expelled all over a fuckin' assumption.

And now, she was in some more bullshit because bitches thought she wasn't 'bout 'dat life. Ari would go to bat wit' anybody: mommas, smart-mouth ass, li'l dusty ass kids, *and* grannies. Shit, learn that she wasn't the one to be fucked wit' and it won't be no problems.

TAUGJAYE

The warden was just done when she walked inside of her office. No more fight was left in her. She was defeated when she saw that Ari had fuckin' ran through the room like a damn tornado.

It was clear that this li'l girl had some anger issues. Issues that were out of her league. With Ari being a danger to the other girls who were living there, when Covenant Housing was designed to be a safe haven, the warden had no choice but to remove the problem. She'd do anything to ensure the rest of the girls' safety, and to her dismay, that was by escorting Ariana Kakos from off the premises/banning her from returning.

***

His phone had rang for like, the tenth time that evening, and Jazlyn was officially ova' it. She hopped up from ridin' Audric's dick and slammed the bathroom door behind her while she let him handle his business. It was *obviously* more important than she was.

First, it was Dutch's death that had him so busy and emotionally disconnected from they relationship.

Then, it was hoes stepping to her while she was at the mall, talm' 'bout how she was fuckin' her man.

And now, King Pharaoh had some new product out. It had the crackheads penny pinchin' even worse than what they already was, and a nigga on his team stayed needin' to re-up.

She was so sick of his shit, and at this point, the fuckin' money he was footin' her wasn't even worth it anymore.

Releasing an unbothered sigh, Audric ignored her for a li'l minute while he grabbed his iPhone from off the nightstand.

It was Tress.

"Yo'?"

"Them all-whites just came in, bruh."

Code for, they new shipment was at the trap.

"Bet. I'm in the county. I'mma meet you thur'."

"Bet. I'm still on the north handlin' a li'l sumn', so I'mma fuck wit' you in a minute."

Audric hung the phone up. He took a few gulps from his ice water before he headed to the bathroom after Jazlyn. He was thankful for Tress, man. Wit' Dutch gone, work was stupid heavy, and his cousin was on his shit. Tress picked up a lot of slack. He knew his boy had enough on his plate wit' his position right up under King Pharaoh, and Audric straight appreciated that. In this shit, you was only as good as yo' team, and after pluckin' a few weeds, he knew shit would run smooth wit' sells.

This street/beef shit was already heavy, and they couldn't lose on the money end.

Fuck that.

Jazlyn, aka J-Lyn, had slid her Victoria's secret lingerie/teddy back on. She was now standing in front of the mirror throwing some flexirods in her micros. They were gettin' old and she'd need them redone pretty soon.

"Bye, *Audric*."

He chuckled at her wannabe hard/mad ass wit' the lick of his lips.

Jazlyn was a fine ass redbone wit' a nice fat ass that drove Audric wild. Her titties weren't too big, but that was cool wit' him 'cuz he was an ass man anyway. She tried to act like she wasn't fazed by his fine ass standing behind her in the mirror and almost gave in when he licked his lips again.

"Nigga, just leave. Don't get mad when I get me anotha' nigga that wanna fuck wit' me and spend some real time wit' his bitch," the Adrienne Bailon look-alike, minus the Latina background 'cuz Audric liked his bitches a hunnid percent Black, spat as she rolled her eyes at him.

"Fuck you say to me?" He growled as he sexily grabbed her by the back of her neck and bent her over the sink.

Audric used his teeth to rip the new, extra-large, Gold Magnum open. He rolled it on and glided the tip of his fat, ten-inch dick up and down her middle.

"AB!" J-Lyn cried when he entered her from the back and shoved every inch of his rod in the depths of her pussy.

"Bend yo' ass ova'."

His St. Louis twang and the way it rolled off his tongue made her eyes cross. Jazlyn was originally from Houston before her peoples made that big move when she was seventeen. She'd been hooked on his ass since the first time she heard him speak. She planted the palms of her hands flat on the mirror while standing on her tippy-toes. Audric held her by the hips and started jammin' in that pussy while her ass jiggled wit' each thrust.

"Fuck, AB!"

"You goin' wur'?"

It was more of a statement rather than a question as he smacked her on her ass. J-Lyn's moaning filled the air as he reached up and grabbed her by the front of her neck once he pinned her back to his chest. Audric stuck his tongue in her mouth as she rotated her hips on his dick while he played in her pussy too. She was always claimin' how she was leavin' him when she knew good and damn well that she wasn't goin' nowhere unless he said so.

"Turn around," he commanded out of breath.

Audric stood back and made sure the condom was still secure as she hopped up on the edge of the sink. Jazlyn spread her legs for him wit' that look in her eye. He smirked at her cute ass while patting the head of his dick on her pussy lips—monents before he entered her and put her legs on his shoulders. He then reached up with both his hands and grabbed her perky, B-cup titties. They spilled from her teddy due to the way he was hittin' her shit; he pinched her nipples.

Half the time, J-Lyn didn't understand what this nigga did to her or her fuckin' mind whenever he had his dick inside of her. All she *did* know was that he knew how to make her feel good. He knew how to make her pussy coat his condom wit' all that silky white shit that she produced when she was satisfied. No otha' nigga had done that to her before, and it was part of the reason why she couldn't leave his ass alone for good.

Audric held her right leg back by her head. He watched as his dick went in and out of that pussy while he fucked her to a moderate pace. Real shit, he wished he could lay up wit' her and fuck her all night. She had some great brain too, but he had shit to do. So he picked up his speed, causing Jazlyn to hit her head on the mirror each time he reached her cervix wit' a forward thrust, but she ain't care.

Audric bit down on his bottom lip and choked her when he felt that nut fill the condom. He shook his head in disbelief while he pulled out, then flushed it before he reached for a clean towel and washed himself off.

Jazlyn stormed off once again wit' anotha' attitude. Quickies meant he had to go, and no matter how much she loved him, even though he'd never told her that he loved her too, she was truly hurtin' by the way he just walked in and out her life. They didn't even date anymore. The best she could get outta his ass was when he would sometimes bring ova' dinner. They'd watch a movie and fuck a coupla' times before he left.

'Dat's it.

She knew Audric was busy, but he wasn't even makin' a effort to show her that this is where he wanted to be, and that's what killed her.

"Straighten up yo' face," he asserted while buttoning his Burberry shirt wit' the sleeves that he always wore rolled up to a quarter length.

"No, 'cuz you steady treatin' me like I'm a ho and not yo' girl, AB."

He liked how it sounded when she called him AB versus Audric. When Audric came out her mouth, she was on some otha' shit tryna be his mama, and he ain't have time for that shit.

No, he couldn't stomach the thought of Jazlyn being wit' anotha' nigga 'cuz they'd been fuckin' 'round since they was seniors in high school, but Audric knew it would never be nothin' deeper than what they already had goin'. He gave her the title of bein' his girl because it shut her ass the fuck up. A real relationship couldn't be forced wit' him. When he was feelin' a li'l breezy on that level, he knew how that shit was really 'posed to feel. It was crazy how he just ain't get that vibe wit' J-Lyn. Nah, it wasn't right that he kept leadin' her on, but for now, it worked, and he was gon' leave it at that.

Jazlyn sat on the edge of the bed wit' her arms folded and her bottom lip poked out. She watched him peel off a good thousand dollas to leave her wit'. Audric stuffed it in her titties as he stood between her legs. He teasingly kissed on her neck wit' those panty-droppin' big lips while he rubbed on her booty. He had *somewhat* of a soft spot for Jazlyn, so he didn't mind givin' her a li'l sumn'-sumn'. A thousand dollas wasn't shit. He could make that back, triple, in one round in a Craps game.

"Go get you sumn' nice this weekend. Send me some pictures after you hit up the lingerie store too. Ia' fuck wit' you lata'."

TAUGJAYE

There was nothing more for them to discuss, so he hopped inside of his brand new 2008 Cadillac XLR and headed back out to the hood just like that.

It'd been a few days since that shit popped off at the burial. That li'l voice in the back of Audric's head kept telling him not to make that detour while he was on his way back to the city. But as he puffed harder on the Kush blunt while knocking off the bottle of Remy that he was takin' to the head, he found himself crossing that bridge, and he was now floating through the streets of Cahokia, Illinois.

Offin' that nigga Syd wasn't enough for him.

Watching that Grand Prix crash and rise in flames was nothin' but a mere crack of the surface as far as he was concerned.

Ain't shit else popped off since the burial, but all that did was tug on Audric's anxiety.

Now niggas was hidin'?

Now niggas was takin' precaution?

Now niggas ain't have that same fuckin' heart to step to him face-to-face about what the real problem was?

And he still ain't have no answers on why his best friend had been murked?

Yeah, okay.

Cahokia was like a ghost town for the most part.

Streets was long.

They were dark.

The dim, orange lighting from the streetlights made the open fields surrounding the roads look like some shit straight up from out a horror movie. It set the tone for what AB had in mind on doing tonight.

He pulled his ride up in a dark shady spot beside a large trash bin and secured the silencer on the nose of his gun before hoppin' out. Quite and discreet, he headed to the apartment complex that wasn't too far away in distance. For it to be a Friday night, he was surprised how chill it was.

The hood was silent like a church mouse.

His right mind kept telling him to turn around and take his ass back to his own damn hood. Enough blood had been shed up until this moment, but the buzz from the liquor had finally kicked in, and now the nigga was a walking animal camouflaged in a human façade.

Moonie rolled her eyes when the knocking on the other side of the door boomed over her TV. Her kids had already stopped her fifty-leven times while she was tryna finish up these fuckin' box braids and get this girl out her house. She was already feelin' a way after findin' out her baby daddy, Syd, was murked. Shit hit her hard when she got that call about STLPD identifying his burned up body inside of a crashed car. She was pregnant wit' they fourth baby, and now, ten times as emotional knowin' that her nigga was gone.

All she wanted was a clear head.

To fuckin' relax.

She was already dealing wit' pre-eclampsia during this pregnancy. All this other shit did was piss her off, stressing her out even more on top of what she was already battling.

Suckin' her teeth and rollin' her eyes, she hurried up and finished the braid she was on before stompin' ova' to the door. Moonie was so fuckin' irritated that she didn't bother to look out the peephole first. The moment she unlocked the door and attempted to pull it open, the person on the other side of it shoved the bitch ajar hard as fuck. The impact from it smackin' her in the forehead and splitting her shit wide open caused her to hit the floor.

Audric let off one round from his untraceable burner, sending blood splattering across the living room wall. The bitch gettin' her hair done didn't even stand a chance.

He'd be lyin' if he said he felt sorry for shorty gettin' caught up in the crossfire of a fuck nigga's sloppiness—in the remedial way he'd been movin', but AB only knew how to keep it real. Syd paved a way to jeopardize his family's safety the moment he decided to cross him, so in a time like this, the last thing Audric would eva' do is show mercy.

Moonie groaned just above a whisper as she rolled ova' on her back and felt her forehead where the blood was trickling from. As her vision cleared, she damn near jumped out her skin when she saw the nigga standin' ova' her wit' a ski mask and a black hoodie on. He had the gun aimed right between her eyes.

She was thankin' God that she'd put her kids to bed, not even ten minutes ago, before this shit had happened. She'd rather it be her than them any day.

Audric walked around to the side of Moonie and popped a squat. He grabbed a handful of her fire-cracker red hair and held the gun up underneath her chin while starin' into her tear-filled eyes.

"I don't know nothin'. I swear," she sobbed while her body started shakin' uncontrollably.

He chuckled.

He admired her loyalty to her fuck nigga ass baby daddy, but she was automatically a target as a casualty of war. She could try her best to plead her way out this shit all she wanted to. He ain't give no fucks.

"Come on, Moonie, mane." AB chuckled while playin' wit' the toothpick in his mouth. "I know you betta' than that."

"AB?" she questioned with fear on the tip of her tongue.

"In the mu'fuckin' flesh, bitch, and I ain't got time to be goin' back and forth wit' yo' ass eitha'."

She pissed on herself when he placed the barrel of his gun against her stomach, knowin' he'd pull the trigga' wit' out even thinkin' twice about it.

"Tell me what I wanna hur', Moonie."

Audric was known in the streets as a cold-hearted killa'. Moonie remembered the conversations her and Syd used to have. Ova' a blunt, they'd rap about the way this nigga shut shit down and how he moved like the hood's neva' seen it before. Even the King was impressed wit' how his solider grazed these streets. Nigga was a certified heavy-hitta, and Moonie knew not to push his buttons when he was already weatherin' up a storm.

She'd fuck around and have her mama and kids on the 5 A.M. news if she went against him. She knew betta'.

Tears streamed down her red cheeks as she silently apologized wit' her thoughts for what she was about to do, and that was go against the grain and disrespect her nigga, to save herself.

Audric could easily see it in her eyes, knowin' she had too much to lose if she kept her mouth shut.

"R-Runo. He was puttin' somethin' together wit' Runo about the Bloods takin' ova' yo' set. That's all I know, AB, I swe—"

Phew!

Moonie's head jerked back as the bullet lodged through her skull and entered the floor before she could finish. Audric shoved her away from him and stood up. He didn't remove the gloves he was wearin' or the ski mask and hoodie until he was crossing the bridge back into St. Louis. It was the perfect opportunity to toss it out into the river and get rid of the evidence.

Now he had a solid enough name and was that much closer to solvin' this fuckin' puzzle.

5

"BEST TO BACK UP 'FOR I SEND YOU A LICK,"

−DIAMOND

Audric was leanin' against the hood of his ride, sipping from an ice-cold Corona when Tress pulled up. He parked right behind him. AB could see two shadows behind the dark tents from the help of the streetlight right above the windshield. But what he didn't expect to see was a wild-haired and highly aggravated Ari swing the door open. It flew ajar so fast that she almost rammed it into the pole that was near.

"Aye, I'on give no fuck how mad yo' ass is. Don't destroy my shit or else we gon' have a mu'fuckin' problem, Ari!" Tress scolded right before she slammed the door and took off on foot.

Audric messed wit' the toothpick in the side of his mouth as his eyes switched from Ari's ass in her booty shorts, to his li'l cousin who wore a scowl on his face.

"Let me go take her shit inna' house first, and we can handle dat. Ari got da' right one wit' all dat attitude shit."

Audric's face remained stone. It didn't twist or turn—an indication that he knew Tress was leavin' out some vital information. He knew he ain't like that shit. AB had practically raised this man his whole life. He knew what his bullshit looked and sounded like from a mile away.

Defeated, it made Tress sigh as he ran his free hand down his wrinkled face.

"She gon' be stayin' hur' wit' us fa' a li'l minute. Just until she get her bread up and she can move into her own li'l spot when she turn eighteen. It'll be a li'l ova' a month. I'mma let her take my room and I'mma chill in Te-Te shit. I already laid shit down wit' her hot ass, so she know what it is. She ain't got nowhere else to go, man. I know she wild den' a mu'fucka, but I can't leave her hangin' like dat."

One thing Audric always respected about Tress was the way he spoke wit' finality. Wit' his head up.

Authority.

Courage.

Bass.

Surety.

Tress wasn't a pussy about shit. If he believed in somethin', he stood for it. AB brought him up right and was proud that he was able to steer Tress in the right direction—no matter how crooked his life was. So he didn't press the situation. They had more important shit to be worried about and would handle first things first.

As Tress headed inside, Ari had already made her way up the block to 12th street. Hot, steamy, and aggravating tears cascaded down her face as she approached Leah's door. She hadn't heard from nor seen her best friend since Yvette dropped her off at the girls' home, and Ari needed a shoulda' to cry on for once.

She was miserable.

She was hurting.

She wanted some consoling and needed to hear that everything was gon' be alright. Tress was so busy actin' like her damn daddy versus her best friend these days, and it was really startin' to irk the fuck outta her. Ari knew Tress meant well. She understood what he was doin' and where he was comin' from, but right now, she needed that brotherly love. Not that hip shit he was on, and for that reason, she'd just chill wit' her girl until she calmed down and was ready to turn in.

Ari felt like she'd been knockin' on the door for forever in a day until she finally heard the lock unlatch. Ms. Yvette stood before her wearin' some real sexy shit. Her hair was all fresh to enhance her look in her Victoria's Secret lingerie, in hopes that her man had finally arrived. So standin' face to face wit' Ari was not only a disappointment, but it even pissed her off a li'l bit to see her there.

Maybe it was all in Yvette's head that Audric ain't wanna have shit to do wit' her like that no more. It was just strange how he ain't been answerin' her calls and how he wasn't tryna fuck on the nights when he knew she was off.

"What'chu doin' hur', Ari?"

Yvette rolled her neck while bringing the skinny and lumpy blunt up to her lips. She wasn't the best roller on the block, but she did what she could so she could smoke her trees.

"What's wit' all the attitude, Ms. Yvette? I ain't did nun' to you. You ain't neva' had no problem wit' me spendin' the night eitha', but alla' sudden you on some real brand new shit."

"Who the fuck you think you talkin' to, Ari? You lucky you Leah li'l 'supposedly' friend, or else—"

"Nah, you lucky you her mama, or else I woulda' been split yo' mouth open. 'Cuz you beefin' wit' me all ova' what? A nigga I ain't neva' had a full-blown conversation wit'? You too grown for that shit."

Yvette blew a gust of smoke in Ari's face, and it took everything in her not to pack off on her friend's mama.

"That was yo' last warning, ho! Try me! Really fuckin' try me! 'Cuz wit' the way I'm feelin' right now, Ia' beat the brakes off yo' ass!"

Ari was mad as fuck. By now, she was punching her left hand between every word she spoke, hoping it was this bitch's face. This woman was on some straight-up bullshit, and Ari had had enough of this shit for one day.

But Yvette was unbothered. Homegirl was as cool as a fan as she took another puff of her Reggie wit' a menacing smirk on her face.

"At the end of the day, you on my property, li'l wanch. So jump stupid if you want to. I'll have yo' ass locked up and in the jailhouse across from City Hall. I'm glad we movin'. You been fuckin' up my daughter head for the longest, and she don't need no li'l ho-ass friends like you around. Because of yo' ass, she can't go off to college and do sumn' betta wit' her life. Yo' hood-rat ass ways dun' rubbed off on her. Get the fuck off my front and don't eva' bring yo' ass back while we still hur' or call my damn phone again! Yo'—"

"Oh, shit!"

The li'l niggas a few feet away chillin' on they generator was amp. They had been watchin' them chop it up since Yvette had answered the door, and they had a feelin' that Ari was gon' square up. She bucked Yvette dead in her mouth, splitting both her lips like she promised, before grabbing her by the hair and started dragging her down the walkway. Ari's adrenaline was so high that she couldn't hear nun' around her. She'd blocked out everything but Yvette's screams as she continued to drag her down the concrete that was getting marked wit' her blood. Her skin was breaking from the brutal force and friction that Ari wouldn't let up on.

I mean, shorty was straight man-handlin' this bitch like she wasn't her friend's mama, and right now, she just ain't give no fucks. The rage was so heavy that Ari just started stompin' this old bitch until she felt somebody pull her away and keep her from fuckin' Yvette's old ass up.

"Let me go! That bitch all mu'fuckin' bark and no bite once she start gettin' her ass beat! I'm sicka' y'all hoes! Y'all old hoes! Ya' young hoes! Leave-me-the fuck-alone and keep my name out yo' fuckin' mouth! Straight up!"

"Aye, calm yo' ass down, and I ain't gon' say that shit again."

The voice serenading in her ear wasn't familiar, but it wasn't unrecognizable eitha'. It was as if the rush she was just feelin' had faded away and was gone wit' the wind. It was crazy how she acted once she realized that it was *his voice*.

Tress was the one pickin' up a hysterical and bloody Yvette off the ground, wit' her bitch ass. So when Ari looked ova' her shoula' and saw Audric hovering ova' her, it's like she succumbed to his stature.

To his authority.

Just like that, the wild beast that lived within her went right back into hibernation while she tried to slow her breathin' down and relax.

"Get that bitch off my property! Right fukin' now before I call the police!" Yvette yelled as Tress tried to pull her back in the house.

All of a sudden, she had some energy and wanted to act tough like she ain't just get her ass beat, instantly flippin' Ari's kill switch back on.

"I got yo' bitch in my trunk, ho! Wassup?! You know you was foul for that shit! That's why you so fuckin' embarrassed 'cuz you ain't think I was gon' do shit off strength of Leah! Disrespect gets no passes wit' me, ho! You just mad don't nobody want that dry, prone to getting' a yeast infection every otha' week, funky ass pussy you got—you ole' daily-douching ass bitch!"

Laughter broke out from the crowd standin' around observing ery'thing go down, and it did nothin' but embarrass Yvette even more. She'd be the laughingstock of the hood for weeks and was grateful that they movin' truck would be there on Sunday.

"Didn't I say calm yo' ass down, Ariana? Huh?"

So many wires in her jumbled brain had crossed from the sound of his clit-throbbing voice that Ari ain't know what to do. The nigga was smelling good, even wit' the beer on his breath since he'd been drinkin'. The way he held his arms around her petite frame, pinning her back to his chest, had her head all ova' the place.

Her pussy juices was churnin'. Her love button throbbed so hard, she could feel her racing heart matching the tempo. She could hear the shit profoundly in the depths of her ears. So much so that, it drove her crazy and would've turned her into a lustin' ass psycho until she finally came back to her senses.

"Audric, you ain't my fuckin' daddy! Get yo' ass off me! You the reason why this ho felt so fuckin' comfortable steppin' to me in the first damn place! Keep yo' hoes in check! I ain't even checkin' fa' you, and yet I'm still a got damn target! *Let-go!*"

She tried her best to break free from his grasp, but all that did was make him tighten up his grip. Audric wasn't the type of man to play into a woman's bullshit, and that was very clear while Ari continued to fight. It wasn't until she finally called it quits and calmed down, did he finally let her go. But the last thing he was expecting for her to do was to turn around and smack fire from out his ass. I mean, his head jerked completely in the opposite direction! She fuckin' bitch-slapped the shit outta him.

"Bet yo' ass take yo' got damn hands off me the next time I say so, nigga! Won't you?!"

***

"Aye, you a'ight?"

Ari looked ova' her shoulda' when she heard Tress' voice. She was laying in his bed watching her favorite movie, *Money Talks*. It'd been a few hours since the shit wit' her and Ms. Yvette had popped off. The hood was still goin' crazy ova' that one, but she could care less. Ari knew that Leah would neva' forgive her. She went overboard by putting her hands on her friend's mama and that she also knew.

Her anger and violent behavior was worse now than it's eva' been. She was just tired of being a target. Hate was one thing, but Ari felt like people were blatantly attacking her. After nonstop years and instances of the nitpicking, altercations, and senseless fighting, she became overly defensive.

Easily offended.

Neva' eva' was she tryin' to fall victim to or play like the whole world was out to get her, but facts was facts, and she was ova' this shit.

"Yeah, I'm a'ight."

Tress entered the room and sat on the edge of the bed. He pulled a half-smoked blunt from behind his ear and handed it to her along wit' a lighter.

"You sure?" He couldn't help but laugh when Ari cut her eyes at him. "Chill out, Laila Ali. You know how I am when it comes to you. I just wanted to make sure you was a'ight before I left to go make this move."

"Tress, go get you some damn pussy and quit worrying 'bout me. I'm good. Yvette's old ass asked fa' that shit, so it is what it is at this point. If Leah don't wanna fuck wit' me no more 'cause she gon' take her momma side, then I gotta' live wit' that. I'd chose my momma too, so…" Ari hit the blunt and let the smoke release through her nostrils before she shrugged her shouldas.

For the first time in her life, she was speechless, so she left it at that.

Tress wasn't gonna press the issue. Ari was his left hand. He knew her. She was in a mood and didn't wanna get sentimental about anotha' dilemma she was battling. Giving in, he walked ova' to her, kissed her forehead, and told her he'd be back in the A. M.

Roughly twenty minutes later, the doorbell finally rang, indicating that her IMOs pizza was there. She didn't bother to acknowledge Audric, who was sitting on the couch getting faded and playing the game, nor did she bother to look in his direction.

What did they have to talk about?

"Keep the change," she commented before closing and locking the door.

Without bothering to say excuse me, Ari crossed in front of the big-screen television, causing Audric to lose his mission on GTA.

"Damn, man! Yo' rude ass betta' start using yo' got damn mouth like you got some fuckin' sense, Ari. You too grown fa' all that attitude shit."

"Mind yo' fuckin' business, Audric, and I'mma keep minding mines. Don't come at me like that 'cause yo' ass lost. You gon' learn quick that I ain't like nun' of these St. Louis bitches that bow down to yo' ass," she spat in return.

Nigga think 'cause he slang dope that he some-fuckin'-body. Boy, bye.

But Ari soon had a rude awakenin' when she felt him come up behind her. He grabbed her by the elbow and rammed her into the nearby wall so fast that she ain't know what to do. And he ain't give no fuck about making her food fall on the flo' eitha'. She was lucky the shit was still in the damn box.

"Audric!"

Ari choked up when he wrapped his hand around her neck. Was she mad as fuck that this bitch ass nigga had the audacity? Hell fuckin' yeah, but she was also equally intrigued. Had it not been for the evil glare in his low, red eyes, her pussy woulda' squirted, and she didn't even know what the fuck that was!

"Let me tell you sumn', li'l hot-shit mouth ass girl. You in my shit. I'm the king of this mu'fuckin' castle, this block, and this fuckin' city! I'on give no fucks about how cool you is wit' Tress. When you see me, get yo' mu'fuckin act right! I murda' hoes out hur' too, in case you think I'm some pussy ass nigga, so it's nun' to smack one eitha'!"

"Boy, bye! Ia' cut yo' mu'fuckin' dick off in yo' sleep if you eva' think about puttin' yo' hands on me! You just mad, like I said, 'cause you ain't shit in my eyes, and a bitch like me won't neva' give you no play! So you can 'I'm the king of the castle—' these nuts, my nigga!"

It shocked the hell out of Ari when he laughed in her face. And not that, a'ight, I was playin' kinda laugh, eitha'. Audric shook his head in disgust and let her simple-minded ass go. She wasn't worth the effort, not even on her best day.

"What makes you think that I'd eva' want a childish ass li'l bitch like you, Ari? Huh?"

She couldn't hide the tears that immediately rushed to the surface of her eyes. Did he really just say that shit to her?

"Aw, so you embarrassed?" He smirked. "Then let me finish. Do it look like I'd be out hur' caught dead wit' a li'l young ass bitch who workin' out people's kitchens? You don't own shit but a sour ass mouthpiece, ma. You break even to make it to the next day when the bitches I associate wit' got businesses and careers. You ain't got shit I want. You ain't 'em woman and mature enough to stop letting these hoes provoke you.

TAUGJAYE

Ery' li'l thing a bitch say to you, offend you. 'Cause at the end of the day, them hoes still in school and got a place to stay while you out hur' down bad. You weak-minded, you stay bothered, and you think 'cause you kinda-sorta cute that people 'spose to fall in line?" Auric laughed so hard in Ari's face that tears slid down her cheeks. Embarrassed wasn't even the word. "Fuck outta' hur', li'l silly ass girl."

There was no use in continuing. He knew she was too emotionally affected by *how* he said it versus *what* he said, to comprehend his words. Ari had a lot of growin' up to do. If she thought that this is how she was gonna get by in life, being a rude ass bitch to everybody that she crossed paths wit', then she had anotha' thing comin'.

6

"IT'S GETTING LOUDER, GIRL, CAN'T IGNORE IT NO MORE,"

–MARIO

Ari's head ain't been right for the last three days. Nobody had eva' stepped to her like that.

Talked to her like that.

Hurt her damn soul like that.

Not in a long time.

Audric had her triggered and not physically.

His every disrespectful ass word had been beating the forefront of her brain, and it had her all ova' the damn place.

"Fuck! Oh my God, AB, baby, yeeeeessss! Shit! Shit! Shit! Ugh, gimmie all that dick!"

Ari wanted to kill this nigga.

She knew this was his crib, but the least that nigga could've done was warned her before he started fuckin' some bitch in the next room ova'.

TAUGJAYE

A streak of jealousy had her too deep in her feelings.

She had a headache from hearin' his headboard knock against the wall no matter how loud she turned the TV up.

Ari wanted to fuckin' cry; shit, *had been* cryin' behind closed doors non-fuckin'-stop, but that shit ended now!

Or, at least she tried to convince herself that shit.

She didn't know why it hurt so bad to know he was makin' some otha' bitch feel good.

Ari didn't like Audric!

Did she?

"Man, fuck this shit. I ain't finna sit in here listening to them fuck all morning!"

Quicker than shit, she threw on a red Hollister jogging suit with some wheat Polo boots and made sure to slam the door as hard as she could on her way out.

She had nowhere or no one to turn to.

Leah called and left a nasty ass message on the phone Tress was letting her use, and Ari was sick. She could hear the hurt in her best friend's voice despite the cussin' and screamin'.

Ari was fuckin' wrong for that altercation, and no matter how many text messages, voicemails, and phone calls she made to plead her case, Leah didn't wanna hear it.

Lately, Ari found herself ridin' the Metrolink from one starting point to the otha', on both the Red and Blue lines, to try and clear her head.

The shit didn't work.

If it wasn't for the iPod Tress gave her, she wouldn't even have the music in her ears to calm her.

Every sex song that came on made her stomach hurt. All she could hear in her head was that bitch moanin' Audric's name and it fired her the fuck up!

I don't even like that nigga!

Ari wasn't a good liar at all. She was too real of a bitch for that shit, but it sounded convincing. That eternal debate went on in her head until she found herself in Pawn Lawn County. Ari had a cousin who owned a hair salon on the corner of Jennings Station Road and Natural Bridge.

She hadn't seen Missy in years come to think of it. None of her momma's side of the family had really fucked wit' them like that since Alivia chose her man ova' her peoples. Shit, she was surprised when they showed up at the funeral.

Ari knew it was bold as fuck to be walkin' up in Missy's shop like this, but what else did she have to lose?

All heads turned towards the door when the bell rang. It was no secret that Ari was pretty. Even with only eyelashes and lip gloss on, she was the shit. Her hair was styled in two Mickey Mouse curly buns with the back down. She always smelled good. Her momma's favorite perfume was Burberry Brit, and it's all she wore. It made her feel close to her momma. No matta' what her money looked like, she'd drop her last at the mall for a new bottle.

She had to.

Missy put the marcel hot irons down when she recognized her li'l cousin. They used to be close. Missy was ten years older than Ari and used to babysit her all the time when she was little. Family beef had torn them apart, but none of that shit mattered when Ari ran into her arms wit' tears in her eyes.

"Damn, li'l cuz. I hate that you goin' through this shit. Leroy ain't neva' been shit, wit' his bitch ass, and these niggas and bitches in this city is straight-up wicked."

They were sitting in the break room now. Ari spilled her mu'fuckin heart out to her cousin. It felt good to get that shit off her chest, but it ain't change shit. She was still stuck like Chuck.

"Wicked as fuck. It's like, I don't know what the fuck to do. I'm tryna get this money for a spot, but it ain't happenin' fast enough," Ari vented.

"It ain't gon' happen ova' night, cousin. That's life. Long as you stay focused, you can do whateva' you put yo' mind to. I tell you what."

"Man, Missy—"

"Bitch, shut up. I got a whole booth available. I ain't hurtin' for the money. I might not be able to offer you a place to stay, but I can help you get yo' money. Tress might mean well, but he sell dope for a living. If he ain't buying you no crib cash, then you need money on paper to get a place. You stay yo' ass outta trouble and keep that bullshit away from my shop, then as soon as you got the move-in money, Ia' co-sign for you and get you some fake stubs.

Don't fuck up my name, Ari. I know Granny Anne and yo' momma turnin' in they graves right now seein' the shit you goin' through. Keep yo' shit togetha' and Ia' hold it down. I still love you, and I'mma always love my Te-Te. It's almost been a year since she died, and I know you hurtin'."

Ari swallowed her cries and blinked back tears. The shit felt weird as fuck when people tried to help her. According to the world, she was a fucked up ass person, but God kept comin' though right when she needed it.

She promised to pray tonight.

Shit was rough fasho, but it coulda' been worse.

"You for real, Missy?"

"Nah, bitch, for fake."

Damn, it felt good to laugh.

"I 'preciate you, cuzzo. I swear."

They hugged it out.

"It's all good, baby. Today yo' lucky day. I gotta walk-in, too, and she want a bob. Get out here and make this money. Ia' give you some supplies to start off wit'. We ain't gon' let this devil win, and that's on our granny grave."

***

Ari ain't expect to make so much money today. She made it to Missy's around noon and left at nine wit' roughly six hunnid dollas in her pocket. The shop was jumpin' today. Every walk-in she got, she had them in and out of her chair in no time, and since she was in a shop now, she could charge a li'l mo'.

Man, she was thankful.

Her cousin still had a few mo' heads to go that night, so she had her man drop Ari off at home after she stopped at the grocery store.

Of course, the KL was crackin' when she got there. Nobody had eva' seen the bad ass Harley Davidson F-150 in they hood before, so you know all the niggas and the bitches was talkin' shit when she hopped out the front seat.

Tress was shooting some hoops wit' his squad when he saw her get out. He'd been blowin' her up all damn day but figured she'd come home when she was ready. Wit' his shirt off and his ball shorts hangin' off his waist a li'l bit, he used his shirt lyin' on the ground to wipe the sweat from his face. He then headed towards the truck but was stopped by the black Escalade that pulled up on him.

It was King Pharaoh wit' Audric ridin' shotgun.

They all chopped it up ova' business as Ari used her key to get in the house. What she didn't expect to see when she walked in was some light skinned bitch in her panties, cookin' noodles like she lived there.

J-Lyn was just as surprised when she saw Ari. 'Cause who the fuck was this bitch?!

"You rude," she spat when Ari sat the groceries down on the counter without speaking.

"And you must be out yo' got damn mind. Put some fuckin' pants on. You don't live here, ho."

"Neitha' do you!"

"Actually, I do. Didn't you see me use a key to get in here? Yop, I'm the pretty bitch that sleep next door to yo' nigga. I'd feel a way too." Ari smirked while walkin' off.

Ain't no way she gon' let Audric get off wit' fuckin' this ho earlier when he knew she was there. She owed him and this Cheetah Girl lookin' ass bitch that.

Like Ari suspected, that bitch ain't want these hands. She showered in peace and changed her clothes before getting some dinner started. Her white rice was boiling and a second batch of fried chicken was comin' out the grease when Audric and Tress made it in.

"Niggas got it smellin' right up in hur'. Oooh, and you made yo' gravy, girl?"

"Tress, gone." Ari smiled when he stole a piece of chicken.

"Where you been?"

"In my skin. Anything else, my nigga?"

"Yeah, you almost got that nigga kilt," he commented about the dude in the F-150.

"That was Missy's nigga since you keep cryin' about it."

"Missy? Y'all back rappin'?"

Ari nodded her head yes as she plated two thighs and a leg, some Uncle Bens, green beans and turkey meat, and a croissant for him.

"I'mma need to get Manda's ass ova' hur' to take notes." Tress grinned as he watched her smother the chicken in gravy.

He loved his bitch, but the only thing she knew how to do was pop some pizza rolls in the microwave, so just know that he was about to bash.

"Who is she, AB?! Huh?! Some random ass bitch got a room and a key, yet I don't?!"

J-Lyn's voice carried from up the stairs as she lost her cool ova' nothin'. Ari wanted to run up there and drag that bitch by them crunchy ass micros, down the steps. Her hands were shakin'. She wanted to react so damn bad, but for some strange reason, Audric's words kept running across her mind.

"You ain't 'em woman and mature enough to stop letting these hoes provoke you...you weak-minded, you stay bothered..."

A mixture of emotions filled her. It's like a bunch of stupid ass math symbols was ricocheting in her head. She was soooooo disorientated.

And Tress just stood back chewin' his food in disbelief. This girl dun' beat her fists on the counter, slammed a few drawers, and drank her apple juice like it was a shot. In fact, she grabbed the fifth of Hennessy from out the cabinet and threw some back!

Might've gagged on it, but she swallowed it.

His friend did everything *but* lose her temper and explode on Jazlyn.

Nigga could've fainted.

"The fuck got into you?"

Ari cut her eyes at that nigga so hard, he reached for his throat to check for blood.

By time Audric was done checking Jaz, Ari and Tress were seated on the couch bashing shit when they made it downstairs.

"Let me catch you tryna make a move on my nigga. You know yo' name get around, ho. I'll beat the breaks off you ova' this one."

Ari damn near snapped her neck when she looked in that ho's direction. The hand holdin' her fork was shakin'.

An awkward silence filled the room.

Tress put his plate down to prepare to break up a fight, and AB stood there staring at Ari, waiting on her to reply.

But she never did.

Instead, she busted out in laughter, forking another spoonful of rice and gravy into her mouth.

J-Lyn didn't know why Ari's reaction pissed her off so bad, but she was floored when Audric shoved her out the door. Like, literally, and *then*, closed it in her face.

He didn't even kiss her goodbye!

Was he feelin' that bitch or sumn'?

He'd neva' done no shit like that.

Jaz banged on the door for a good five minutes, but Audric ain't answer it. Her car ride home was a sad one, but if he thought she was brushing that shit off, then he ain't seen nun' yet.

***

"Wake up, nigga! We goin' to Miami!"

Tress snatched the covers from off Ari so got damn hard that her scarf came off.

"Yo', what the fuck, Tress?! You fuckin' up my hair, and it's too got damn early in the mornin' for this shit!" she yelled wit' an attitude.

"I'on give a fuck about nun' a that shit you talkin'. You got a hour to have yo' shit packed and be ready. We got a plane to catch."

Ari rubbed her temples and sighed as his rude ass slammed the door behind him. Fuck a damn Miami. It might've been her weekend off since Missy was expecting the state to come through. Shit, she needed a damn break too since she'd been workin' nonstop for two weeks now, but she was tired. I mean, dog-dead tired.

It was ova' though when Tress barged back in the room five minutes later and pulled her by the ankles until her body hit the floor. She punched him in the damn mouth before screaming, "What the fuck is wrong wit' you, nigga!"

"I said get yo' ass up!" he screamed while putting her in a headlock.

Ari elbowed him in the nuts to get free then body-slammed his ass. Their laughter filled the air when he shoved her from off of him.

"A'ight, you WWE Smackdown wrestler."

"Fuck you, Tress," she giggled. "You know I'm crazy."

"As fuck. Get ready though. We been out hur' grindin' like a mu'fucka. Let's go get drunk and kick it. Consider it an early birthday celebration."

Now that Ari was fully awake, she realized that the idea didn't sound half-bad. She'd never left the city before, nor flew on a plane. She didn't know if it was the excitement or her nerves that had her shakin' in the backseat of Audric's Escalade.

Speaking of that nigga, she ain't know his ass was comin'. She was surprised to see that his prissy ass Cheetah Girl wasn't glued to his hip for the trip. Tress invited Manda to go too, so she wouldn't be the only chick there. But Ari wasn't dumb; this had to be a business trip. It had King Pharaoh's name written all ova' it, but it was free so she kept her mouth closed and went wit' the flow.

Tress hadn't seen his best friend this got damn happy in a while. Like a kid in the candy store, she was snappin' pictures wit' her camera of the beautiful city until they made it to they hotel. She hadn't complained not once since his extra ass wakeup call a li'l minute ago. The only thing she asked was if he could take her to the nearest mall so she could get some clothes to fit the weather, and her wish was granted.

"I ain't tryna be all up in yo' business, Ari, and you know I don't want no beef," Manda started while poppin' her gum.

TAUGJAYE

They was in Aeropostale lookin' through the swimwear. Tress and Audric were handling business, so they were havin' a li'l girls' moment.

"Nah, I don't fuck wit' Audric." Ari laughed. She was high as fuck right now, thanks to the Kush they got on the plane via a vitamin bottle. For once, she was in a chill mood. "Tress woke me up on some, 'We goin' to Miami,' shit, and I was like, okay. Me and Audric barely say two words to each otha' around the house. It ain't no beef, but we just don't fuck wit' each otha' like that. And trust that a bitch ain't losin' no sleep ova' it eitha'."

Y'all know Ari wasn't no friendly ho, but Manda was cool peoples. She graduated from Triple C last year, and they'd always got along.

"Mmph." Manda smirked as she turned her lips up.

"Mmph, what?"

"I hear what chu' sayin' an all, but wit' the way he been lookin' at chu' all mornin', it seem like he like what he see. They say his dick big. Even if you don't fuck wit' him, bitch, what happens in Miami stays in Miami, okay?"

Aru busted out in laughter.

"Bitch, you funny. That's the funniest shit I dun' heard all year."

"Ari, I fuckin' know you. Quit playin' wit' me. You know I ain't no sketchy ass bitch, first and foremost. And second, if I was you, I would give these bitches somethin' to fuckin' talk about since they keep yo' name in they mouth. He tryna play that shit off, but real recognize real. J-

Lyn woulda' been hur' if he really wanted her to be. And just between me and you, he don't even claim her like that.

She clingy as fuck and begs him to come around. Yeah, they fuckin' and he might give her a coupla' dollas from time-to-time, but Tress say he don't even like her like that. They just been fuckin' for so long that she his numba' one round. Sit on that nigga's dick and have fun. I would if I was you. That's how I bagged Tress."

Ari ain't know what to think.

She ain't know what to say.

Manda might've had a point, but Ari's cherry wasn't popped. Even if she "did" agree to take it there wit' Audric, he'd probably clown her about bein' a virgin, and she ain't have time for him to be embarrassing her. That was somethin' that he seemed to like to do to people. She could see his ignorant ass laughing at her now. Nope. Ari was good.

"Nah, Manda, I'm straight. Mu'fuckas already think we fuckin' now. I'm just out here tryna get my paypa' and nun' else."

"Exactly why you should fuck him! Ugh, you suck a li'l loc. I'mma have to school yo' ass. That's how I know bitches just be talkin' on yo' name 'cause you straight a good girl out hur. 'Prolly still a virgin, too."

"Bitch, don't be sayin' that shit out loud. The fuck?"

Their laughter filled the air as they continued to shop. The swimwear in Aeropostale was a'ight, but it ain't have shit on what the Bebe store had to offer. It was over when they stepped foot in there. Ari bought her whole wardrobe up in that bitch, blowin' almost a stack.

TAUGJAYE

I mean, *did* Audric have an eye for her?

When Tress handed Manda ova' a good 10k in cash, Audric turned around and did the same for her. He didn't flash a smile, try to push up on her, threaten her about payin' him back, or even look her way wit' that crazy ass glare in his eyes.

Nigga forked ova' the cash like it was nothin', and Ari ain't know how to feel. *Was* he gonna want it back? *Was* he just frontin' 'cause they was outta' town, and he had to show niggas why he was king?

Ari tried not to look too far into it and convinced herself that this must be how it go when you friends wit' niggas who got money. But then again, Manda's ole' loud-mouth ass had to put that damn bug in her ear. On the real, this was too much, honey, but it was his dime, not hers.

***

King Pharaoh had a large shipment comin' in between today and tomorrow. A shipment so fuckin' large that Audric and Tress would be driving that shit back to St. Louis in U-Haul semi-trucks themselves. Yeah, they came to Miami to get away for a few days, but when it was all said and done, every move they made was calculated.

Money was flowin' like water. Audric had been flippin' so many bricks, his dick stayed hard the whole time he counted his weekly profits.

But on the flip side?

Bodies was droppin' like flies in them St. Louis streets. After Syd's BM came up murdered, it's like a petty ass war had started. Niggas from

AB's set were gettin' popped, and for each one of his soldiers that fell, his locs doubled up on the snoops.

AB was leavin' that mark ass nigga, Runo, for last. He knew Moonie wasn't just talkin' shit before he blew her brains out. She'd always been solid. That nigga ain't showed his face in the KL since Moonie's death.

Fucked up move on his end.

That alone had let Audric know that nigga knew sumn' about Dutch bein' murked. And as much as he wanted to act off impulse, AB had to take his time and map this shit out just right. He was gon' avenge his potna's death soon enough. That shit would go down in the streets to further paint the picture of the legacy that Dutch left behind.

They made it back to the beach in no time after making sure that shit was squared away for they rides back to the Lou. Audric and Tress had money. Long fuckin' money. When you continued to make 30-40k a week, you was eatin', my nigga.

So it was nothin' rentin' a charter yacht wit' all naked and fine ass BLACK bitches to wait on them hand and foot. Manda had just texted Tress and let him know that her and Ari had finished gettin' dressed. They now was headed to the beach to meet them.

After takin' a piss, he went to find his cousin.

AB was chiefing on a fat ass blunt stuffed wit' that good Kush while one bitch rubbed his feet. Anotha' was massaging his shouldas, and in his free hand was a bottle of top-shelf Moét.

Aye, they *was* on vacation, right?

"Niggas ain't waste no time." Tress grinned as he dapped his cousin up.

"Nun', bro. The heat been so mu'fuckin' hot in St. Louis. It feel good to not have to look ova' my shoulda' ery' five minutes."

"I straight feel you, bruh. I'm goin' balls-deep in Manda's shit, twenty-fo-sem' while we hur'. I need to release that stress, you hur' me?"

Audric chuckled, flashing the dimples you'd neva' know he had 'cause he rarely smiled. Him and Tress chopped it up over your average male banter for the next fifteen minutes or so until they felt the boat take off. He pulled the blunt from his lips when Ari came into view.

She wore so much weave, he neva' would've thought she had the hang-time that was pulled up high on her head. The red, Bebe, two-piece that tied around her neck was sick on her body. Ari was built like a grown fuckin' woman: slim and juicy in all the right damn places.

She had a few basement tattoos up and down her left arm, one real big on her thigh, and a tramp-stamp that read, ARI, with some wings on eitha' side of. Shorty honestly didn't even need makeup. Audric was a li'l glad that she wasn't like the otha' chicks around the hood who was jumpin' on that trend.

He didn't like the fact that she drank though. It rubbed him the wrong way, but shit, he wasn't her daddy. He ain't know why it did sumn' strange to him to see her smilin' so much eitha'. Maybe she needed this break just as much as he did, and he wouldn't knock shorty for wanting to have a good time.

It was startin' to get cold back in their hometown, and they was poppin' bottles on the coast of Florida. They was about to live this shit up for the next forty-eight hours wit' no inhibitions.

TAUGJAYE

7

"YOU KNOW THAT YOU'RE FEELIN' THIS TOO, SO LET'S KEEP IT REAL,"

−CIARA

Whateva' Manda had the bartender put inside of this mystery ass punch had snuck up on Ari, quick. Maybe if she was back in the hood, she'd keep takin' these cups to the head. But she wasn't. Plus, *he* was watchin'.

Damn, Manda wasn't lyin'.

Ari sipped on a bottle of water as she used a brochure to fan herself. It was in the low-nineties that day, a li'l humid, and her baby hairs was curlin' up. Lil' Boosie's voice was blarin' out the party speakers, setting the mood for their jam session. She bobbed her head to the beat but felt herself freeze up for a minute when his track "Set It Off" started playin.

This. Was. Her. Shit!

Ari got too hype.

Thanks to the liquor, she was feelin' the heavy bass in every limb of her body. Shorty was about to cut it up. Wit' her white oversized Christian Dior shades shielding her face, that she just had to cop earlier, she was fine as hell jiggin' to the beat. Manda joined her in the area that they'd designated as the dance floor. She wasn't necessarily pop, lockin', and droppin' it, but Ari was shakin' ass. Real cute-like, she dropped it down to the flo' wit' a new drink in hand, thanks to Manda. She stuck her tongue out and looked back at her booty bouncin' while her girl's drunk ass hyped her up to her favorite part of the track.

"We real niggas wit' G-codes!

Love to go in beast mode!

We thuggin'!

We all got bread, so if we fall, then we the crutches!"

Even Tress and Audric had to hop up on their feet for those four crucial ass lines. When you was a real ass nigga, you understood real ass shit. When you came from nothin', from the gutter, then you appreciated yo' day-ones and yo' grind on a whole 'notha' level.

The mix playin' in the background was tryna' get some shit started. That "Sexy Can I" by Ray J and Yung Berg came on, and the atmosphere changed.

Ari was drunk out of her young mind. Not to where she was about to be throwin' up, but her hormones? Audric knew what he was doin' lookin' at her wit' the bottle up to his lips. He was too fresh in Burberry swim trunks, a matching short-sleeve button-down that he wore open wit' no undershirt, and matching slides.

Rollie doin' numbers in the sunlight that beamed down in *it*, and the VVS diamonds in his ears.

Maybe it spoke a bit of his language the night Ari laughed in J-Lyn's face. Maybe he was proud of shorty for goin' out and landing a job in a shop. He ain't know how she managed to finesse that, but shit, it was sumn'. Her sudden productivity might've made his dick hard knowin' she'd heard *and* understood him on the night he checked her.

She still had a stank ass attitude like he wouldn't pop her ass in the mouth. Shit, she was true to herself, but he knew she was frontin' to hide the fact that she had a thang for a hood nigga.

For the oh so famous, Audric Bowden.

Ari started cheering Manda on when Tress came up behind her. Home-girl was throwin' that ass like she wanted the dick right now, and Tress ate all that up.

It startled Ari when Audric stepped to her. He backed her into the railing and looked down at her while he continued to swig from the bottle.

Her heart was racin'.

If she weren't wearing shades, he'd be able to see how wide her eyes had grown. His glare was so fuckin' intense though. Ari ain't wanna come off like a li'l scary ass bitch, so she was smooth wit' it when she turned around and started grinding on him.

Yooooo, is that this nigga's dick?

Ari couldn't hold her laughter in. She dropped her head, dipped it down a little low, and kept rotating her ass all ova' his package. She saw why that li'l hatin' ass Cheetah Girl was screamin' so damn loud when she was getting fucked the otha' day. And Ari didn't even have to fuck him to see that!

"That's my dawg!" Manda cheered, imitating Smokey from *Friday*.

She knew after a few drinks that her girl would loosen up.

Audric knew he ain't have no business fuckin' around wit' Ari like this. This li'l girl was gon' have him out hur' on some otha' shit. Some shit bitches prayed they could share and experience wit' him.

Especially after living wit' her these last few weeks, and he realized that she as far from what the hood made her out to be. Seventeen was legal in the state of Missouri. Plus, she'd be eighteen in three weeks, too. He was far from a nasty ass, Chester ass nigga, so gon' head and get them thoughts out ya' mind right now.

They was already bein' accused of fuckin' around. First, Ari's fight wit' Ms. Yvette, and now she had a key to his crib. *They* might've known what it was or what it wasn't, but that ain't mean shit compared to how it looked.

Yet, no matter how you spun it, Audric was a grown ass man. He was gon' do whatever the fuck he wanted to do and who he wanted to do it with—as long as it was ethical. He could care less about what nan' nigga said or thought.

It was his life.

TAUGJAYE

"So you *can* listen," he whispered in her ear.

Ari had butterflies. She couldn't believe she was in Florida wit' the biggest drug dealer in town. Not to mention he had his arm wrapped around her waist. I mean, a girl can dream, but to experience this shit in real life?

Baby, she was floatin' in thin air.

"And *you do* know how to speak my language, huh?" was her reply.

Audric raised a brow at her sassy ass.

At the li'l cute way she rolled her eyes and fluttered her long lashes. Sumn' about a hood bitch wit' swag and bamboos made him a slave to 'em. Ari had the whole package. Once she got all her ducks in a row and started thinkin' bigger as far as her future, she'd be untouchable.

The bitches would really be hatin' on shorty then.

Man, he could see all the drama now if he started fuckin' wit' this girl.

Was it worth it?

"You gon' make me fuck you up wit' this smart ass mouth, shorty. Chunk."

Ari smiled, matchin' the one he was flashing her with. A chill ran down her spine when he licked those plump and juicy lips. The gold grill behind them sent her ova' the edge. Ari leaned in and kissed Audric. Eitha' he'd be wit' it or not, but he surprised her, once again, when she felt him slip his tongue between her lips and kiss her back.

Ari neva' expected a nigga like him to be so damn affectionate. Audric was kissin' her like he'd been holdin' this shit back, and it had her nub twitchin', glitching', and thumpin' to where she thought she came.

Lord hammercy, God!

And it didn't stop there. AB showed Ari a good ass time that day. She'd neva' ridden inside of a Ferrari before. Ari couldn't explain how much fun she had—how special she felt to ride beside him in the two-seater. They smoked and floated down the freeway wit' Tress and Manda behind them.

Her pretty long tresses was blowin' in the wind, she had her shades on, a smile covered her face, and she was snapping a million pictures on her red Sony camera. Everybody had a camera in 2008. That was given!

Audric was fine as hell spittin' the lyrics to Lil' Wayne's verse on Lloyd's "You" as he whipped in and out of traffic. When he reached ova' and gently stroked her chin, Ari melted into the leather seats.

A bitch like her read books about this shit. She'd always imagined herself being Gena in *True to the Game* by Terri Woods.

On Quadir's arm rockin' wit' her dope man. It was funny being hur'; even if it was only for a coupla' days.

They were stuffed after a lobster and steak dinner come nightfall. In a matter of hours, Ari had a taste for the finer things in life. Applebee's would always be the MVP in her book, but there was always room to add somethin' new to her list of favorites.

When they made it back to the hotel, Tress didn't hesitate to get Manda back to they room so he could blow her back out. Audric needed to smoke anotha' blunt before he called it a night, so he grabbed Ari by the hand and led her outside. The beach lined the back of their hotel. With all of the string-lights hangin' ova' the pavement, he took the opportunity to walk the shore wit' shorty as they passed the green.

"Thank you, Audric."

He looked down into Ari's eyes when she handed him the smokes back.

"You finna get all soft and shit on me now, shorty?" He chastised wit' a smile that blew her away.

His fuckin' dimples swooned her.

"I'm just keepin' it real wit' you." She blushed. "You said some shit that I needed to hur'. You was right. I mean, I still wanted to bash yo' damn head in the wall, but I couldn't deny the fact that you was spittin' some real ass shit to me."

Audric chuckled as he took a deep toke from the blunt.

"I see you started getting' yo' shit togetha', too."

"Real shit, I did. I got me a day scheduled where I'mma take my GED so I can apply for hair school and get a license. I can't keep workin' in my cousin's shop wit' out one, so I'm tryna hurry up and get that done. I ain't tryna get her in no trouble wit' state just 'cause she doin' me a favor."

"Word?"

He was surprised to hear that. Ari really was out here tryna get her life back on track. Tress was right: she just needed some guidance.

"Yup. Ain't nobody obligated to do shit for me. I gotta make it do what it do. I swear I'm not what you been thinkin' of me."

"And how you know what I think of you?"

"Audric, I'm not slow. I might be a lotta' shit, but I'm far from dumb. You thought I was a rachet ass, ain't shit ass, li'l bitch out hur'."

"A *ghetto* ass, ain't shit, li'l bitch out hur'. I can't 'em lie, but a nigga neva' accused you of being a rat when I knew you ain't move like that."

Ari laughed. She'd let him get that shit off today. She was feelin' too good to argue wit' his blunt ass.

"Check it," he continued. "You sumn' to hate on, Ari. You sumn' to brag about, and can't no nigga in the KL, the Peabody, The New Houses; shit, in the whole damn Lou say that he fucked you. Can't no nigga say that you dun' ate dick. That shit piss haters off, shorty. Continue to build up yo' immunity to the bullshit. The loudest nigga in the room be the softest. Remember that shit."

She nodded her head in agreement as they continued on down the sidewalk. Shorty loved when he laid her off wit' a good word or some good game. Nigga ain't neva' told her nun' that she couldn't lata' use.

It was creepin' up on the midnight hour. North Beach would be closing as soon as the clock struck twelve, and Ari wasn't ready to turn in just yet. The experience and the view was beautiful. A project chick like

TAUGJAYE

Ari could only dream of being this close to the fuckin' ocean. *And* it was peaceful too. They spent a lot of time during the day on South Beach where all the action was.

Audric was a low-key ass nigga. Yeah, he was gon' pop out and kick it where the parties was jumpin', but when it was time for him to wind down, he liked his peace. The solace calmed him. Reason why he always stayed at the St. Regis Bal Harbour Resort wheneva' he touched down.

You couldn't beat the tranquility of a beach-front hotel wit' out all that otha' shit.

You just couldn't.

He pulled Ari into his lap after taking a seat on a beach chair that someone had left out. She wrapped an arm around his neck. The kush swirled in his lungs the longer he continued to inhale from the Swisher Sweet.

Ari couldn't take the way he was starin' into her eyes. Smoke clouded his face as the dim light-post beamed down on them. She found herself runnin' her thumb along his naturally arched eyebrow, sexily leanin' her head ova' to the side as she bit her bottom lip.

Audric grabbed her by the back of her neck wit' his free hand and pulled her close. He stuck his tongue in her mouth, causing Ari to moan from his panty-dropping aggression. It came too damn natural the way she mounted this man's lap wit' out breakin' their kiss. Her body was heatin' up. Sensations were striking her lady-parts with so much rage, she couldn't help the way she started grindin' on his bulge.

Audric put the blunt out so he could use both hands when he started rubbin' on her back and grippin' her ass. All she wore was a bandeau and booty shorts. His hands graced nothin' but skin as he started kissin' on her neck.

Ari had to keep it one thousand.

She'd neva' been this intimate wit' a nigga before. Yeah, she'd dealt wit' a few niggas throughout high school, but she'd neva' allowed one to get this close. Ari saw what a man did to a woman when she fell in love wit' him. Leroy and her mama showed her at a young age what toxicity looked like, and she neva' wanted to let a man have that kinda' power ova' her.

Hell, she hated when a bitch stepped to her on somethin' reckless, so why would she allow a man to treat her like shit?

The world looked different, shit, a whole lot different when you was raised on survival and not love. It ain't that she didn't know how to love, but Ariana Kakos would neva' be played like a fool.

Especially by a sucka' ass nigga.

Shit was different wit' AB, though.

He touched her like he loved her.

Shit might've sounded a li'l ova' the top, but this nigga gave her butterflies. It was every girl's dream to find them a romantic, hood nigga.

Audric had been openin' doors for Ari, was cashin' out, kept his tongue in her mouth, always wanted to hold her hand or drape his arm around her shouldas.

TAUGJAYE

I mean, yeah, it might've only been a day, but niggas didn't fake the funk for a bitch he ain't want. Audric was too cocky to waste his time and money. *That* she'd known about him for a well-known fact. It's not like she hadn't weighed the possibility of Audric playin' her.

He was that nigga and she was a project chick.

There was a difference in havin' insecurities and being secure.

Survival was her M.O. Shorty wasn't the easiest to finesse, but she had to admit that he had her right he wanted her, and she was all game to continue.

Ari couldn't help the way the moans kept seepin' through her lips as he gnawed down on her neck. She already knew a hickey would be left behind.

Her nipples blossomed when he pulled her top down before takin' one into his mouth. It was a mixture of passion and hunger that exuded from his every motion, and it had her pussy wet. Ari rubbed on the back of his head as his tongue flickered ova' her saturated nipple. A shock ran down her back again, causing her to squirm in his arms as she watched him latch onto her like a child.

Her body reacted to him like he was callin' out commands, and that shit made Audric's dick grow harder. Again, younger girls wasn't how he rocked because he needed a bitch wit' a certain mentality on his arm, but Ari? It was sumn' about li'l momma that made him hold back—think twice.

It was sumn' that made him ponder about the coulda's if you placed their names in the same equation. That shit said a lot in itself, okay?

Ari blinked and he had her laid on her back, trailing deep kisses down her stomach. AB let the tip of his tongue twirl around her navel until he made it to her zipper. It was obvious by her body language and energy, by the way she panted and rubbed on his silky waves, that she wanted him to keep goin'. In seconds, he had her shorts off. In seconds, he was kissin' the inside of her thighs until he made it closer to the pussy that he was about to put in his mouth.

"I'mma do this shit for these next coupla' days while we out hur', but when we get back to the Lou, you gotta get this shit waxed, shorty."

Ari covered her face wit' her hands and giggled from the embarrassment. She ain't have no wolf-pussy, but it *was* a li'l thin mink coat down there. Shit, she was a virgin! Waxing was the last thing on her mind. Her shit ain't stink, and it was clean, so in her eyes, she was doin' good.

Nervousness filled her when she heard a coupla' voices in the distance. A couple who was on they honeymoon was passin' them by, but it was clear that Audric ain't give no fucks.

Did he ever?

He was drunk, he was high, and the moment he inhaled her pretty pink clit between his lips, my dude went ham. Ari's back arched and she instantly forgot about someone possibly seeing them. That shit went out the window when his tongue started gliding along the aisles of her pussy.

She screamed his fuckin' name at the top of her lungs. She might not have been experienced, but eitha' a nigga knew how to eat pussy or he didn't.

The head was gon' feel good or it wouldn't.

There was no in-between.

Her body trembled from the notion of him gliding his tongue up and down her middle. When he zeroed back in on that sacred spot and showed it nothin' but relentless love and attention, Ari felt somethin' inside of her ignite, somethin' tingle.

"Fuck, Audric..."

Her very-first male-induced orgasm had swept ova' her, and Ari was fuckin' in love wit' this nigga now.

No fakin'!

He literally was slurping her juices out of her chamber while they continued to pour down, and it drove her insane. But when she felt him slip a finger in her pussy, she immediately tensed up—never knowin' what an ounce of vaginal penetration had felt like until then.

"You a virgin?"

Embarrassment was written all ova' her face when she looked down and they made eye contact. Audric ain't neva' felt no pussy this damn tight. Not since he first lost his own damn virginity ten years ago. Yeah, he'd been gettin' around for a li'l minute.

"Y-yeah..."

She was almost scared to admit it, just knowin' he'd get all pissed off and go fuck a random Miami ho versus dealin' wit' this shit. But the smile that covered his face made her heart skip a damn beat.

Ari ain't know what was happenin'.

"What?" she asked wit' nervousness on the tip of her tongue.

AB chuckled wit' the lick of his lips. His dick was throbbing from the taste of her that was still left ova'.

"You sure you wanna' share that wit' me?" was his next question.

And as a matter of fact, Ari *wasn't* so sure. She'd be crushed if he got back to the Lou and started playin' her. Thoughts of him runnin' back to that fuck ass Cheetah Girl straight pissed her off that quick. He could see it in her eyes that she was thinkin' the worse, forcing him to laugh again.

"I ain't gon' hurt you, Ari. I mean, my dick will once it start stretchin' this tight ass pussy out, but I ain't gon' break yo' heart. I fucks wit' you."

"So, you like me?"

"Ain't that what I just said?" He countered.

"Audric, speak clear and concise English to me. Okay, nigga?" She giggled.

He loved how her chubby cheeks rose wheneva' she smiled. Ari was sexy as fuck to him to be honest. A pretty li'l brown thang that he could now call his own.

TAUGJAYE

"If I ain't like you, Ari, you wouldn't 'em be hur'. Real talk."

"So, wassup wit' chu and yo' li'l Cheetah Girl, then?"

Audric screwed up his face before saying, "Man, what?"

It took him a li'l minute to figure out what the fuck she was talkin' 'bout. That is, until he thought of J-Lyn. Nigga dropped his head and laughed at that shit. This girl was wild.

Shorty straight called this bitch a Cheetah Girl, fam. I'm hollin'.

"Let me handle 'dat. That's my fight, not yours."

"Nigga, I'm not—"

"Aye."

AB was puttin' a stop to that shit before she could even get it started. He knew where she was goin' wit' this, and right now, that shit wasn't 'em relevant.

"If and when I say sumn', Ari? Take my word for it. If I say I'm gon' handle that shit, then that mean I'mma handle it. J-Lyn *think* she my bitch, but she ain't. I ain't even the type of nigga to explain myself, so that should already let you know where my head at. I'm eatin' yo' pussy, Ari, *and* it's hairy. I'on just do that shit fa' fun."

She busted out in laughter while clappin' her hands togetha'. Yet, he thought *she* was wild.

"You know we finna' start some shit wit' this one, right?" She commented with a real sexy smirk.

"Wit' what?"

"Wit' you bein' my nigga."

AB chuckled. He'd be lyin' if he said he didn't like the sound of that. Shit kinda rang a bell. Ari was a cocky and confident ass bitch, and he dug that about her. She needed a lot mo' guidance and enlightenment, but for the most part, she was solid. She valued the shit he said. Ari listened to him, and we all know her ass ain't listen to nobody.

A gal' who was willing to submit, learn, and improve was a gal' worth puttin' his time into, and in this very moment…AB accepted the fact that this li'l girl had him in the palms of her hands. And he was cool wit' that.

"You mean, wit' you bein' my bitch?"

A smile graced her face like she was smilin' for her third-grade school pictures. This nigga had jumped the gun wit' her, coining them as an official couple. When Tress told her to consider this trip as an early birthday gift, she neva' woulda' thought that hookin' up wit' Audric would be the icing on the cake.

"Man, get yo' goofy ass up and let's take this back to the suite. Nigga can't be poppin' yo' cherry and shit on no lawn chair…you deserve betta' than that."

8

"I WISH YOU WERE HERE,"

-JAMIE FOXX

Ari should've been proud of herself. It took her a week to study for and pass her GED. Two weeks, wit' that last one included, to get herself enrolled in cosmetology school. She was nervous as fuck during her interview. Paul Mitchell was the best academy in the state.

Her interviewer was white, it was a predominately white school, and the location was smack-dab in the heart of the city: The Central West End.

The KL ain't look shit like the area where Audric had dropped her off at on her first visit. All she could think about was these uppity ass white folks turnin' up they faces and judgin' her. She was even more nervous knowin' her situation wit' the expulsion, but God was showin' out in her life like neva' before.

Ari kept it real wit' the gay dude that interviewed her. She ain't lie to try and make it look like she was an angel. She gave him a minimal on her background, let him know that she was in a different place than the girl she was when she got put out, and how she was tryna better her life.

Her honesty won him ova.

Her transcripts from Triple C were fuckin' bomb. Ari might've had a few behavioral problems, but she was a straight-A student. Shorty was far from dumb. Shit, she woulda' graduated at the top of her class if she ain't get put out.

She was accepted into their program under one condition: no fighting.

They didn't wanna hear shit out of or about her wit' some drama, or she was gone.

Ari couldn't even be mad. She knew she didn't have the best reputation around St. Louis, but she *was* ready to change the way people saw her. I mean, people was gon' talk shit regardless, but she promised to work on further keepin' her attitude in check to keep from adding fuel to the fire.

Shorty felt productive.

She went to school Tuesday through Saturday, worked at the shop on the weekends, and minded her business. She was on her school shit, and her nigga was getting money. Life shoulda' been gravy right now, but it wasn't.

It'd be a week until her eighteenth birthday.

A *whole-fuckin'-week* until it'd been a year since her momma died.

TAUGJAYE

Ari was numb.

She was hurtin'.

Shorty did what she had to do while she was at school, but come 5:00 P.M. when she got out? The bitch came from out of hidin' and she was a monster.

She'd been drinkin' more.

Way more.

Ari had been sending Crackhead Don up to the liquor store every evening for a week straight. The MD 20/20's weren't doin' it. That shit tasted like Kool-Aid compared to the pain she'd been feelin'. 4Lokos and Hennessy was the only thing that evoked the hurt in her heart, but mentally? It had shorty gone.

Today was Sunday, and she usually cooked a big dinner for her, Audric, Tress, and Manda, but Ari was so drunk and outta her mind that she couldn't even see straight. She was stumbling like a high ass junkie wonderin' the streets in the early mornin'. Just a knocking shit ova' and holdin' her breath ery' time she felt like she was gon' puke.

Her head was bangin'.

The dizziness that had control of her body had her periodically blackin' out. She'd come-to right before she could lose her balance, but wasn't so lucky this time around. Ari tripped ova' her feet and hit the cabinet so hard that she split the wood. Her chest was heavin' up and down so bad that she could feel herself catchin' spasms.

"Oh—"

Ari could feel the throw-up rushin' up her throat, but it wouldn't come out. It hurt so bad. Physically and mentally. She kept beatin' on the center of her chest and on her stomach, tryna force the liquor out. Tears was streamin' down her cheeks; she was screamin' and hollerin', beggin' God to rid her of this shit, but it seemed like her pleas fell on deaf ears.

"GOD, HELP ME! PLEAAAAAAASE, HELP ME!"

Ari was runnin' around the kitchen in circles, pullin' on her hair and pullin' at the shirt she was wearin'. Just goin' crazy. She felt possessed. Her sadness soon switched into rage and she lost it. Shorty started throwin' shit. Pots and pans started makin' musical noises against the ground, raw steaks went flyin' in the air along wit' the now bruised potatoes that she didn't know how she managed to peel; dishes, knives, trash...

She went on anotha' one of her wild ass rampages until a loud voice pierced her ears.

It was Audric.

He ain't know what the fuck was goin' on, but he had his choppa out, ready to body whoeva' it was in hur' tryna hurt her.

But she was alone.

"GET AWAY FROM MEEEEE!" Ari screamed when he tried to walk up on her.

"Put the fuckin' knife down, Ariana! What the fuck is wrong wit' you, cuz?!"

TAUGJAYE

That had to be the worst thing this nigga coulda' said. Them was fightin' words. That shit had set Ari off, causin' her to run up on him. She was swingin' the blade like her name was Michael Meyers.

"I'M NOT THE FUCKIN' PROBLEM! ERY'BODY ALWAYS TRYNA MAKE IT SEEM LIKE I'M A FUCKIN' PROBLEM! I AIN'T PUTTIN' SHIT DOWN, BITCH ASS NIGGA!"

Audric jumped back just in time or else she woulda' drove that blade right in his chest. She was quick too. Her arms moved so fuckin' fast that you could hear the knife whisking in the air.

Ari was chasin' him around the living room like he was the one who murdered her momma. All she saw was red. Spit was flyin' out her mouth as she continued to scream at the top of her lungs.

Man, Audric was pissed.

I mean, HEATED!

He ain't do shit like this. He avoided toxic ass bitches like this for a reason, and Ari had very much shown him that he made a huge mistake by fuckin' wit' her.

'Cuz this shit wasn't about to be goin' down.

Yeah, they mighta' kicked it out in Miami, but he already let her know on the way back in town that he ain't fuck wit' her drinkin'. Audric ain't wanna control her. Again, he wasn't her fuckin' daddy, but that hard drinkin' and fightin' shit he wasn't puttin' up wit'. The last thing he needed was a target on his back via the bitch he fucked wit'. He was already a hot commodity on his own.

"AUDRIC, STOP! GET-OFF-OF-MEEEE!!!"

He had her face smashed into the couch wit' her arms behind her back. His white, long John shirt had blood on it. She'd managed to slice him across the chest before he could tackle her.

"I ain't got time fa' this shit, Ariana! You can get yo' crazy ass the fuck outta hur' wit' all this sh—"

"AAARRRGGGGHHH!"

Vomit went everywhere. All on the couch, all on the floor, and down her shirt. Nothin' but Hennessy and Chinamen came out her mouth, and from the smell, Audric could tell that she was fuckin' drunk. She was throwin' up so bad that he had to hold her hair back to keep it from gettin' soiled too. Shorty was in bad shape, and Audric couldn't believe this shit right now.

"Yooooo. What the fuck goin' on up in hur', dawg?"

Tress walked in on the crib bein' turned upside down and his cousin on top of Ari wit' her hair in his hands. He shook his head in pity when his li'l sister threw up for the thousandth time, puttin' two-and-two togetha'.

"Damn, Ari," he commented with sigh.

And damn was right. She was all the way damned up until the moment she collapsed ova' the edge of the couch and blacked out.

***

A loud groan filled the air when Ari woke up from her sleep five hours lata. After that last haul, shorty was out like a light. Her head felt like somebody had repeatedly punched her in it. For a li'l minute, she just laid there wit' her eyes closed. It was when she realized her hair was a li'l damp that she sprung up in bed, wonderin' what the hell had happened.

The clock on the wall read 1 A.M.

The room was dark.

The television in the background was low wit' clips of the game playin'.

That's when she realized that she was in Audric's room.

It's when she finally realized that he was seated across from the bed in his favorite recliner. His low, red eyes was glued to her.

He wasn't pleased.

She'd fucked up.

She could tell by the look on his face.

Ari inhaled deeply and sighed once she tasted the liquor on her breath. She might not have remembered all of the details right then and there, but she remembered guzzling that Hennessy down the moment Crackhead Don left. No matta' how nasty that shit was, she was so damn mad, she just threw it back.

That, she'd remembered clearly.

Ari crawled ova' in bed until she was able to sit wit' her back against the wall so she could be face-to-face wit' her man.

Well, that's if he still wanted to be wit' her afta' that li'l episode.

She pulled her knees into her chest and threw her head back in defeat.

She'd made a fool of her damn self...

No, she just missed her fuckin' momma.

The tears rushed to the surface of her eyes and down her cheeks wit' out her control. People just didn't understand what she was dealin' wit'. What all she'd been harboring for so many fuckin' years, and it was slowly eatin' away at her core.

"I been wildin' out and havin' this nasty ass attitude for a li'l minute, Audric." Ari wiped the tears from her eyes before she continued. "I ain't neva' been this bad, though...when I was sixteen, I went to spend the night at my uncle's house. Me and my cousin Kina was hella cool. We grew up togetha. That used to be my Ace Boon Goon...Er'body in the family knew her big brotha' was a fuckin' weirdo. Like, the nigga was just weird..." Her bottom lip trembled no matta' how hard she tried to keep it togetha'.

"I swear, Audric, I ain't neva' mean fa' my momma to get caught up in the middle of no bullshit. Like, I swear to you, but the shit was startin' to give me nightmares about what that nigga did to me. I don't give no fuck what kinda' mental disorder they claim that nigga suddenly had. Hell yeah, he was crazy as fuck. Nigga was outta his got damn mind.

He had to be when he snatched me up in his room and tied me down. I'mma fighta', Audric. You know I can bang. You know I whoops ass, but nun' of that shit had mattered that day. Duce was huge, like, three-hunnid pounds huge. Nigga straight tied my arms behind my back and raped me in my ass. Like, Audric, I can't fuckin' make this shit up. The memories be so fuckin' vivid."

Audric wasn't no soft or sentimental ass nigga by a long shot, but the way his shorty sat across from him breakin' down had hit his heart. He put the bottle of water that he was nursing down and climbed in bed next to her. Ari laid her head on his chest when he put his arm around her shouldas. Baby girl cried her heart out. She ain't know how she was gon' get through the next years to come every time her birthday came around. She just didn't. This shit was hard and she ain't know what to do wit' herself.

"And my cousin just sat in her room actin' like she ain't know what the fuck was goin' on. I know she knew 'cause alla' sudden you just hear the TV in the next room ova', which was hers, gettin' louda to drown out my cries. Bitch ain't do shit but let it happen. Shit made me feel like they plotted on me or sumn'. The whole li'l situation was sketchy.

I kept that shit in for like, six months until I started havin' nightmares about it. Like, I was so shocked that shit had happened, I couldn't even react to it in that moment, bae. But when it did hit me, my attitude started gettin' real nasty. I wasn't out hur' pickin' fights wit' people, but I did take my anger out on otha's…

My math teacha' had just called home for the fourth time in one week, and that's when my momma realized somethin' was wrong wit' me. At first, she ain't get it out of me 'cause I was scared she was gon' be on bullshit. You know how Black families be like, *'What goes on in this house, stays in this house.'"*

Ari had to take another deep breath. This shit was killing her to reveal, but Audric let her have her moment. She was grateful.

"I told her though...My momma was fuckin' hurt, Audric. She broke down in tears before she threw me in the car and we drove ova' there. She had it in her heart to kill that nigga. Reason why she called 911 when we pulled up, straight warning them to send the police 'cause she was gon' go to jail for murda. Her and my auntie ends up gettin' into it. At first, her and my uncle claimed I was lyin'.

Then, the bitch turned around and said I probably provoked her son. How he ain't goin' back to no mental homes because I'mma liar. On my life, she pulled a gun out and tried to shoot me. My momma jumped in front of the bullet and her body collapsed right in front of me. My auntie emptied out the clip into her whole body, Audric. I. Swear. To. God.

The police pulled up right when the last bullet went off, and I ain't been the same since. My momma straight got killed tryna protect me. If I neva' woulda said nothin' then she would still be hur'. Like, bae, it's all my fault that she's gone, and I miss her so much. She ain't deserve that. I shoulda just kept my fuckin 'mouth shut. Look at what the fuck I did..."

Ari cried until it put her to sleep, and Audric let her. He ain't expect no wild and outlandish ass shit like that to come out her mouth. That was a lot to hold in. That was a fucked-up ass situation that would

TAUGJAYE

make anybody act out, and he felt for her. He knew shorty wasn't wild for no reason.

Now the drinkin' made sense.

The anger.

The guard she always held up.

The reason why bein' attacked triggered her to lose her shit.

That was a lot on her, and she needed to patch them wounds up or else she'd continue to bleed on the people who ain't scar her.

The next morning came and Ari had a sew-in scheduled for 11 A.M. That was a hunnid and fifty dollas that she'd use to go get her some more black gear for her school clothes. She was still sittin' on a nice pile of cash from the money Audric gave her when they was in Miami. To be honest, her savings was gettin up thur'.

Wheneva' Audric got paid, she got paid.

She was his bitch, so he looked out for her.

He let her use his Maserati when she went and got her driver's license for Christ's sake. Audric fucked wit' Ari. The hard way. It was sumn' about shorty that made a hood nigga's heart race. Nigga mighta' played it off, but he felt a way wheneva' he saw her. Don't let him be on the block handlin' his shit, and he'd see her walkin' by. He neva' realized his feelin's was that deep, or that he felt that way, until they li'l trip.

Ari had him open.

She knew that money was the least of her problems now that they was rockin' togetha'. Audric was far from selfish, but Ari loved doin' hair. She loved tryin' what she was already learning at school on her clients.

It was her practice to make perfect.

Plus, she had a handful of people who only let her touch they heads, so she stayed booked. She was even payin' her cousin booth rent now. Had been compensating her wit' a nice li'l sumn'-sumn' for helping her out. Missy was risking a lot lettin' Ari work in her shop, and it was the least she could do.

The car ride out to Jennings was quiet. Ari was still in her feelin's about how she acted yesterday. She felt like shit for lashing out on her man and cuttin' him. She ain't mean it, and he ain't deserve that. The Lil' Boosie in the background cut the silence he pulled up in front of her job and turned it down.

Ari looked ova' at Audric wit' puppy-dog eyes. He was lookin' at her too.

"Come mur'."

The sound of his voice *alone* did somethin' strange to her. Ari unbuckled her seatbelt so she could lean ova' the console and kiss his lips. It's like he eased all of her tension wit' just the slightest gestures.

"I feel so mu'fuckin' safe wit' you, Audric," Ari whispered wit' her forehead pressed against his.

"That's how you 'posed to feel wit' yo' nigga, ma. If a nigga can't make you feel safe, then he ain't the one. Real shit, I'm glad I can do that for you, though. I ain't that heartless, but I will body the next nigga or li'l bitch that even think 'bout hurtin' you."

Ari smiled so bright, her eyes squinted, and she blushed.

"Thank you, bae. For ery'thing. Thank you for givin' me the chance to explain myself and not just throw me out on my ass."

"Even though that's what yo' wild ass deserved," he started, causing Ari to giggle. Her nub tingled when he pressed those big, juicy lips against hers one last time. "I ain't lettin' you go, girl. Whateva' it is, we gon' thug this shit out. What time you gon' be done?"

"Gimmie like, three hours. She want some crimps, too."

"Bet. I'a be hur' to get you. Keep yo' head up, a'ight? That shit ain't yo' fault. Stop carryin' that weight. Yeah, it's fucked up yo' moms gone, but she wouldn't want you to be out hur' fuckin' up yo' future, eitha'. She gon' always be wit' you. She loved you, and that's why she protected you. That's the shit that you savor, you hur' me?"

Wit' tears in her eyes, she nodded her head like a li'l kid while he cupped her chin.

"Be safe." She smiled after stealin' anotha' kiss.

"Always. Hit my line if you need me."

"I won't hesitate."

***

Mondays wasn't your normal day to get a haircut in the Lou, but Audric's barber would be out of town this weekend for his 20th wedding anniversary. He was an older cat that used to cut his shit back when his pops was still alive, and it's the only nigga he trusted. The spot was crackin' wit' all his clients tryna get in between today and tomorrow.

A lot of them niggas got in they pussy ass feelin's when AB walked through the door. Big Dogg, his barber, tapped the client in his chair on the shoulda' and told him to get up so he could get Audric togetha' real quick.

That's how much weight his name held.

Niggas in St. Louis wished they had even an incline of the money, the power, and the amount of pussy he got. No fakin'. Nigga was such a force to be reckoned wit' that when you thought about the drug game, they'd say his name before King Pharaoh's.

He feared no man and honored God no matta' how illegal his life was. It was one of those things that couldn't be explained. Eitha' you understood him or you didn't. And which eva' side you chose, it made no matta' to him. He ain't give a fuck about the next nigga's opinion. Especially a nigga that wasn't on his level.

Some called it arrogance and he could second that.

Facts was facts.

"'Preciate you, bruh."

"Ain't no thing, family."

"How Ms. Azalea doin'?" AB asked about his potna's mother.

She was gettin up thur' in age.

"Same ole' crazy lady, man. Ain't shit changed 'bout moms but the decade."

TAUGJAYE

"Chunk. I'mma have to go pull up on 'er one day. She gon' cuss my ass out. It's been a li'l minute since I stopped by."

"At least you already know, man. Nobody safe wit' her ass."

Audric chuckled as he slapped hands wit' Bigg Dogg. He slid him four hunnid dollas for the hospitality and hookin' him up. On his way out, AB stopped at the vending machine and grabbed a bag of Sundance hot corn chips and a Vess peach soda. He had to put sumn' on his stomach before he picked his Chinamen up. Nigga was hungry than a mu'fucka.

He'd just hit the automatic start on his Mas when a loud female voice callin' his name caught his attention.

Audric ain't even have to botha' lookin' ova' his shoulda' to know who it was. He thought he recognized her BMW when he pulled up thirty minutes ago. J-Lyn got her hair braided at the Africans right next door to his barber.

Had been since she was sixteen.

It's where they met before he realized they went to the same high school.

"So you gon' fuckin' ignore me, Audric? I knew you was fuckin' that li'l ho ass bitch from the way you shoved me out the damn door that day! You would really do some shit like that?! To *me*?!"

His jaw clenched when she walked up on him, swingin' her arms all ova' the place. He knew this shit wit' J-Lyn wouldn't be easy to break off. Ari struck a nerve for these St. Louis bitches, and him fuckin' with' her for real, for real, gave them all the reason to continue to hate.

On the flip side though, Jaz must've missed it when Audric flicked his nose wit' his thumb. That was a clear indication that he was about to act a fool. AB was a quiet ass nigga for the most part. That's until you pushed the right button to activate his alter ego.

You saw what he did to Syd.

To Moonie and company.

This nigga did not play, and it was very clear that he was gon' have to remind this silly ass girl that shit.

What better to than to embarrass her? Since she wanted to give them bitches in the shop sumn' to see, then that's what the fuck she'd get.

"On my momma, Audric, I'mma—"

Jaz shut that shit up when he grabbed her by the neck and shoved her back against his ride. It's not like he had a handgun in her mouth. Nigga had the barrel of his Draco shoved down her throat, the same way he used to do wit' his dick. Finga' curled around the trigger and all.

AB was just as wild as his bitch was; that's a well-known fact, but let me tell you how fine this psychotic ass nigga was lookin' right now though.

Lining was sit-on-my-face fresh, his dimples were peering through as he bit down on his bottom lip and silently chuckled.

J-Lyn was shook.

Flabbergasted.

Choked the fuck up.

TAUGJAYE

Was hurt beyond this world that he just continued to treat her like she was nothin' to him. In that moment, she realized that she'd wasted seven years bein' this nigga's cum rag. All she eva' was, was a fresh nut.

There was no reciprocated love.

He ain't give no fucks about her.

But he was doin' alla this ova' some young ass, hood bitch who ain't even have a damn pot to piss in?

It ain't get no lower than this.

There was nothing that Jaz could possibly do or say to change the way this nigga saw her. She'd allowed him to treat her like a wild card until it was time for him to pick the right color to win the game.

And it wasn't her.

"They say actions speak louda' than words, ma. White man was right about sumn' afta' all, huh? But check it, let this be the last mu'fuckin' time you eva' approach me. Especially on some ho-shit like this. I told yo' ass what the fuck it was. You knew I wasn't in this shit wit' you like that, yet you insisted. You played yo' self, and keep my bitch name out yo' mouth or we really gon' have a problem. *She* fight, *I* air out clips and put bitches on the news. Rememba' that."

AB shook his head wit' laughter. Exercising his strengths, he shoved her dumb lookin' ass out the way so he could shake.

You see, in his head, Audric was thinkin' that J-Lyn had gotten the message. She must have wit' the way she stood there and pissed through her grey Bebe jogging suit.

But nah. He'd embarrassed and played her for the last fuckin' time. You see, Jaz wasn't dumb enough to swing on a man, but what she was dumb enough to do was to go afta' his bitch.

At this point, the ass whoopin' she was about to give Ari wasn't even about the dick no mo'.

This was about respect.

Her fuckin' dignity.

Revenge.

And she was about to get that shit right fuckin' now.

TAUGJAYE

9

"I NEED A THUG TO HAVE MY BACK. DO-RAG, NIKE AIRS TO MATCH,"

–BEYONCÉ

"Y'all be safe. Don't be gone too damn long," Ari expressed before puttin' a Sugar Daddy sucka' in her mouth.

She thought that her and her boo would be able to chill once she was done at the shop. King was sendin' them to Atlanta this time for anotha' shipment. Trap niggas had to do what they had to do, so she ain't sweat it too bad. Her and Manda was about to go grab a bite to eat down at The Best Steakhouse across from The Fox Theater. She'd been dyin' for a chicken plate. She could already taste their secret sauce that made her lick her fingas clean. Audric was leavin' her wit' the Mas, along wit' a nice fat ass stack of hunnids, so hittin' up the mall was definitely on their itinerary too.

"And yo' ass betta' stay outta' trouble," Tress teased as he walked around to her.

They'd be takin' his whip to the airport.

"Aye, I dun' did a whole one-eighty out hur'. I'mma angel."

Even Audric looked at her ass like she was full of shit. It was inevitable when him and his cousin busted out laughin'.

"Man, fuck y'all," Ari teased.

She stood on her tippy-toes and threw her arms around her man's neck. A chill ran down her spine when he kissed her lips and wrapped his arms around her tiny waist. He was li'l late comin' to pick her up, or else they woulda' had time to get a li'l quickie in.

Ari liked what Audric did to her body. When she said he made her feel safe, she meant that shit. When Foxy Brown said, "Thug Passion," she was talkin' about Audric Bowden. Nigga had the perfect balance of kiss me like you love me, sensual fuckin', and beat this pussy up stroke game, all in one. It hurt like fuck when she lost her virginity to him. Yet, once Ari got the hang of takin' dope nigga dick, the sex was even betta' than the gossip goin' around the hood about him. You see, them bitches was only getting fucked, and Audric actually rocked wit' her.

That shit made a difference.

"I ain't gon' hold you, bae. I got a test to study for anyway. Go 'head. Just hurry back," she teased wit' the raise of her brow.

She was rockin' a high bun wit' some Chinese bangs and a li'l hair on the sides to crown her face. He liked this style on her.

"I got you. I'mma hit you up when we get all settled in and shit."

Ari told him okay and hugged Tress before she went in the house. After starting her a bubble bath, she picked up the phone and did somethin' she knew she shouldn't have done. Both Yvette and Leah hated her ass, but she missed her best friend so much. The shit made her cry knowin' they wasn't talkin' no more. She wondered how she was doin', how was the baby doin', was she talkin' to Dutch's momma about helpin' her raise it, and alla' that.

Ari couldn't just forget about Leah or let her go no matta' what happened. She was willing to be the bad guy and take the fall ova' that fight. She missed her girl and was goin' crazy wit' out her.

"Same ole' cocky and arrogant ass Ariana Kakos. You still callin' my momma phone afta' we both told you to stop. You just don't give no fuck, do you?" was Leah's greeting when she answered the phone.

Ari was surprised that she even picked up. Hearin' her girl's voice had choked her up so damn bad that she could hardly talk.

"Leah, please talk to me," she begged wit' tears in her eyes.

"Why?! You put yo' hands on my fuckin' momma when all we eva' did was try to help you! I rode for you through ery'thing, Ari, and that's how you do me?!"

By now, Leah was cryin' too.

The hurt was heavy ova' they phones.

"And I'm sorry! Ia' be the bad guy, Leah! Nah, I shouldn'a put my hands on yo' momma, but she was wrong! She accused me of sumn' that I didn't even do, and afta' the night I'd already had, that I was comin' ova' to tell you about, I just snapped!" Ari cried.

"Man, Ari, bye. I'on even know what to believe. How alla' sudden you Audric's bitch, then? You fuckin' him now, so life all gravy, and you wanna right all yo' wrongs 'cause it's lookin' up fa' you?"

"Leah, it ain't fuckin' like that! You know I'm not that bitch! That's not how it happened! I been callin' you for HELLAS! Been hittin' you up on Bebo, on Facebook, and alla' 'dat! So don't make it seem like I don't give a fuck about how this shit dun' went too far! Best friend, I miss you! I need you! I'm so fuckin' sorry! Ia' do whateva' it takes to fix this shit!"

Silence stood between them. Ari knew Leah was thinkin' about it. She knew that her friend was missin' her too. They was fuckin' sistas, but it was one thing that stood in they way.

"Leah, get yo' ass off my damn phone usin' up my minutes! It ain't afta' nine, and you bet not be in hur' talkin' to that bitch, Ari, eitha'!"

She could hear Ms. Yvette in the background, clear as day.

"STOP CALLIN' MY MOMMA PHONE!!!" was Leah's last words before the call disconnected.

Ari dropped down to the floor and held her face in her hands. This shit was drainin' her. She knew Leah. Her momma was all up in her ear, keepin' them from puttin' this shit in the past. She'd bet her last mu'fuckin' dolla on it. All ova' a nigga who'd only fucked her a coupla' times? That shit was sick. Ms. Yvette was a grown ass woman wit' a whole ass man out hur'. So why was she trippin' so hard off this shit?

The sound of glass shatterin' made Ari jump up to her feet, quick. She ran into Audric's room and grabbed his Glock 30 before headin' downstairs. Glass was all ova' the living room floor from somebody throwin' a brick in there.

"Bitch, I know you in thur'! Didn't I tell you I was gon' whoop yo' ass, ho?! Come outside!"

Ari instantly recognized the Cheetah Girl's voice. She would've laughed at her dumb, salty, and jealous ass if it wasn't for this mess. This was they auntie house that this bitch was destroyin'. Not hers! This ho was outta' line.

"Bitch, get yo' mad ass the fuck on somewhere! What the fuck is wrong wit' you!" Ari shouted while puttin' on her black Air Force One's that was left by the front door.

Crash!

This bitch threw anotha' damn brick, bustin' out the otha' window.

"Bitch, you my problem! Face me, ho! RIGHT FUCKIN' NOW! I WANT YO' HEAD, BITCH!"

Alla' that tryna' be the bigger person shit went right out the fuckin' window.

Jazlyn had Ari fucked up.

After making sure that the coast was clear in the back of the house, she left out the backdoor, ready to whoop some ass. J-Lyn ain't see it comin' when Ari ran up on her.

Bloop! Bloop! Bloop!

Ari started punchin' that bitch all in the back of the head and in her face, givin' her the hands she swore she was gon' lay on her. The hood surrounded them, goin' crazy ova' how bad Ari was beatin' the brakes off this ho. They ain't know why people liked to fuck wit' her, knowin' she had some mean ass hands that was borderline, lethal.

The sound of police sirens made a large chunk of the crowd scatter like roaches. It took three officers to break up the fight. Jazlyn was a bald head ass scally wag when they finally got Ari hands from out of her hair. Y'all know she loved to drag a bitch to the end of next week. Micro braids was sprinkled all ova' the grass, and ery' part on her face possible was bleeding.

"WHAT THE FUCK HAPPENED TO MY DAMN HOUSE?!"

The voice came from Audric's and Tress' Aunt Angie. She jumped out of her cab the minute she saw the police outside in her front.

Ari stood there in an officer's arms and let out a hard sigh. Everything in her life seemed to go from sugar to shit as soon as she felt like things was on the right track. It's like the whole world was steady plottin' against her at this point. She ain't know how much more of this shit she could take.

"This is *your* home?" an officer asked, tryin' to get an understanding of everything.

"Yes, this is my house! Angeline Bowden! My name is on the lease! What happened to my fuckin' windows?!"

Angie was about to lose her shit if somebody didn't start talkin' right fuckin' now.

TAUGJAYE

"That there girl, Ariana, been stayin hur, Angie," Ms. Jenkins, the hood snoop, explained. She had her cane in one hand and a square in the otha'. "I's the one who called the police afta' this crazy yella' heffa' dun' busted out the first window. She came ova' hur' wit' all this mess, botherin' this girl 'cause AB dun' dropped her like a bad habit. The hood knew he neva' claimed you, li'l girl. Just pathetic."

Ari wanted to cry. Thank God somebody had her fuckin' back for once.

Ms. Jenkins loved her some AB, baby. She'd lie, steal, and kill for that boy. Ms. Jenkins was old school. She knew when a man really cared for a woman, and, baby, he loved him some Ari. Nigga was smilin' more than usual, and her nosy ass knew why. She ain't miss nun' on this block if she was at home.

To look out for Ari and Tress was like lookin' out for him, so that old bird kept her antennas alert.

The police started getting ery'body's statements, tryna decided what they was gon' do. Shit seemed to die down once they arrested Jazlyn for vandalism. Ms. Angie was gon' press charges on that crazy ho if it was the last thing she did. And she loved her nephews and all, but they wasn't right lettin' some li'l ass girl live up in her shit wit' out askin'. She paid them bills. Yeah, her nephews compensated real nice ery' month her for lettin' them still crash there, but this drama shit she couldn't and wouldn't accept.

Ari drove around the city wit' slow jams playin' on the aux cord while her mind raced. As much of her things that she could grab was piled inside of the car.

A blunt was up to her lips.

She wanted to drink so fuckin' bad but knew Audric would kick her ass if he found out. It took everything in her not to call him. Ery'time he turned around, she was in yet anotha' altercation. Ari already knew that Angie had hit him up. That was a given. And she had every right to put her out her house. If she hadn't been livin' thur', nun' of this shit woulda' happened.

Ari thought back to an hour ago when she saw Leroy's ole' bitch ass standin' on the sidewalk watchin' everything go down, too. Nigga shook his head at her the whole time she loaded Audric's car wit' her stuff. He dodged a fuckin' bullet wit' that li'l girl and was glad she was no longer his problem.

"Bitch," Manda answered on the first ring.

Facebook had told her ery'thing just minutes before she called.

"Biiiiiiitch!" Ari was just done. She inhaled deeply from the blunt before respondin'. "Let's talk this out ova' dinner. I need to eat somethin' before I kill a mu'fucka."

"Bet. I'mma meet you thur'. I'm leavin' Grand Nails right now."

"A'ight."

Thirty minutes lata, they was seated in a booth smashin' they food while Ari told her the story. They was halfway through they meals when

TAUGJAYE

her phone rang. It was Audric. She already knew he was gon' have an attitude, so she prepared herself for the next possible twenty minutes of him lecturing her.

"Hello?"

"Man, wassup, shorty? What the fuck goin' on?"

He hadn't even boarded the plane yet. Before he'd even heard from his Auntie, Ms. Jenkins had called him runnin' her mouth, so he knew the truth.

"It's yo' fuckin' Cheetah Girl, Audric. You said you was gon' handle that shit."

Nigga couldn't even take her serious half the time. Ari was sumn' else, but so was Jaz. Now, he'd have to make Ari go whoop her ass again when he got back since she wanted to pull some ho shit like this. Or, he could just kill her fatha'. Eitha' option sounded good to him since she was testin' him like he wouldn't air her parents' shit out.

"We gon' go shoot that bitch, shorty. Straight up."

"See, Audric, you playin', and I'm fa' real."

"Who playin'?"

Ari rolled her eyes and giggled, knowin' damn well that he was serious as fuck. It just made her stomach flutter how down her was for her.

"It's a date then as soon as you get back." She smiled and rolled her neck, even though he couldn't see her.

"On me. Get a pen and paypa out."

She dug around in her purse for it and wrote down the address he told her to.

"Just take whateva' you can ova' thur' today. Ia' get the rest when I get back. Angie all in her feelin's and shit, but I can't even blame 'er. I'mma handle that. Let me know when you make it in. If I'on answa', I'mma hit you back during the night."

"A'ight. Thanks, bae. I'm sorry."

"I know. Don't sweat it, though. You know how these hoes be, but most importantly, you know I got you."

***

That day at the Steakhouse when Audric told Ari to grab a pen and paper, he gave her the address to the mansion in Lafayette Square that no one knew he owned but Tress. Ari's jaw dropped when she pulled up at the five-bedroom, seven-bath, and three-car garage, brick house. It was expected for him to be drivin' some fly shit because of his status. He pushed the Mas when he was in a dapper mood. The Caddie convertible and his Escalade were his run around whips. All in all, people knew he had to be stashin' his vehicles somewhere otha' than on 14th and Park, but he was always in the KL.

It's where he laid his head on most nights throughout the week, aside from when he was out on a power trip. When the nigga said he was low-key, that's exactly what the fuck he meant. Ari had been stayin' thur' for the last three months now. They Auntie Angie had quit her traveling job and got on wit' Delmar Gardens for a Director of Nursing (DON) position, so his crib became hers.

It was the most time he'd eva' spent there since he bought it two years ago. Audric loved his Aunt wit' all his mu'fuckin' heart, but it didn't take long for him to get used to sleepin' beside his shorty. Ari kept him in good spirits. Ms. Jenkins wasn't lyin' when she said that man had been happier. He neva' would' guessed that the love Ari showered him wit' woulda' been somethin' he'd needed.

Somethin' he'd been missin'.

AB couldn't really explain it, but he knew his feelin's for her were deep when she had him layin' up in the house versus chasin' afta' the latest hoes and runnin' the streets. He paid niggas to do a lot of the footwork he found himself drowned in, in the past. The busyness kept him distracted from fallin' in love, but wit' Ari, it was the otha' way around.

The nigga was datin'.

Takin' her on weekly shoppin' sprees.

Getting pedicures and corny ass shit like that because she'd tapped into his heart.

Takin' pictures, lettin' her post about them just a li'l bit on Facebook since she was into shit like that.

Ari had this man's head gone.

Especially right now.

She made it her duty to learn how to ride her nigga's dick. Shorty wasn't stopping until he was callin' out her name like a li'l bitch from the pleasure. She loved to hear him cower from her prowess. Shit made her pussy cream his mans on impact; like it was doin' now.

"Fuck, girl!"

"Audric! Oh my God! Oh my fuckin', God! AUDRIC…"

"Mmmmmmmmph!"

AB bit down on his bottom lip as he held her by the waist and slammed her on his meat wit' force. Ari was havin' anotha' outta' body experience. She threw her head back, her long twenty-six inches grazing the top of her butt as she pinched her nipples and called out in ecstasy.

When Audric felt his nut rushin' to the tip of his dick, he pulled her body close and inhaled one of her nipples. Seconds later, he exploded into the deepest depths of her pussy.

Heavy breathin' filled the air. Their tongues crashed along each other's until Ari collapsed on top of her man. She laid there with her arms around him. One of his hands was grippin' on an ass cheek while he took tokes from his now lit blunt.

This girl was a fuckin' animal on the dick. It didn't take long at all to get her pussy adjusted to his length and width. Ari loved to get fucked to slow jams, and that had been they last few days in a nutshell. After he picked her up from school this past Saturday, they went grocery shoppin' and had been smokin', fuckin', and eatin' ery' since.

She had school in the A.M., and he had anotha' shipment that would be comin' in, any day now. It was back to business, but Audric honestly enjoyed blockin' the world out and chillin' wit' his bitch.

TAUGJAYE

It gave his life balance.

"Did you decide on what you wanna do for yo' C-day yet, bae?" Ari questioned as she carefully reached for the blunt wit' her long nails.

He'd be twenty-four in anotha' month come March, and she couldn't wait.

"You said that like you ain't already got sumn' up yo' sleeve, shorty. You ain't that slick. I know yo' ass been up to sumn'."

Ari giggled as smoke blew through her nose. He was right. She had a bomb ass trip planned to Jamaica. To her surprise, Audric had neva' been out the country yet. What better gift would it be to explore the Jamaican culture as one? It was somethin' they both could knock off they bucket list.

"I mean, yeah, I do," she admitted wit' a smile. "But, just in case you wanted to do sumn' specific, we coulda' made that happen too. You said you neva' really was big about celebrating yo' C-day, and I wanna do sumn' special this time around. You got a lot to celebrate; especially wit' how you held me up and got me through that rough ass week before mines. It's the least that I can do, bae."

He leaned in and kissed her lips the moment she looked up at him.

"Just tell me you luh' me, shorty."

Audric was always chastisin' Ari. He got a kick out of seein' her get thrown off her square a li'l bit 'cause she was so head ova' hills for him.

"You first," she challenged wit' her brows connecting.

"I luh' you, Ari."

Her heart stopped.

Was this nigga really serious?

"Audric, don't fuckin' play wit' me," she declared as she sat up straight, straddling him.

AB chuckled as he ran his hands up and down her thighs. His dick was still inside of her. Her hair was a li'l wild from him grippin' that shit when he had her face down and ass up, drillin' to the core of her tight, juicy pussy.

This goofy ass girl had one of his chains around her neck, too. She was so cute puffin' on the green while burnin' a whole in his ass wit' her big, slanted eyes.

"Why would I play about some shit like that, Ari? I know what the fuck I feel when it come to you. Now, say it back."

Ari blushed as she hid her face wit' one of her hands.

"I love you too, Audric."

"I know."

"Boy, shut yo' ass up!"

A weight had been lifted off her shouldas after exchanging 'I love yous'/ knowin' that she and her nigga was on the same page. She'd loved Audric since that night he sat up and let her cry on his shoulda' about her momma. And the way he made her eighteenth birthday so damn special?

TAUGJAYE

He sent her two dozen roses up to her school: one red bouquet ('cause that was her favorite color) and the otha' was made from one hunnid dolla bills. They went to Panama City that weekend. Had dinner at Ruth's Chris that night. Got a room at the Ritz Carlton, and he let them pamper her at the spa to keep her mind off her mom's death. When they made it back in town, there was a matchin' candy-painted red Maserati in the garage wit' a bow on it.

Audric knew he was wild fa' that one, but this girl had some kinda' spell on him that he couldn't shake. Straight up, and it ain't trickin' if you got it. Nigga was sittin' on millions. Wasn't no need to be stingy wit' his gal.

She honestly was his first real love.

"Shit! This is my soooooong!" Ari squealed when the melodies from the guitar started playin' through the stereo.

AB continued to puff on the blunt as she slightly rocked on top of him, snappin' and singin' to that "Southside" by Lloyd and Ashanti. Ery'time they got in the car, she just had to blast this cut and sing to him. Her day wouldn't go right wit' out doin' so. Li'l hood ass loved R&B.

AB could feel his dick startin' to tense back up. He was ready for anotha' round inside of her platinum coated pussy that had his name on it. Knowin' he was the only man to eva' touch her, minus you know what, made him feel good. That was sumn' else he couldn't explain, but aye, it was true.

Nevertheless, Audric could make out his phone ringin' ova' the music. A groan slid through his lips when he reached for it. Ari was slowly glidin' up and down his pole to the tempo of the song, and if it wasn't Tress callin', he woulda' ignored the call.

"Yo'?"

"Pull up. Them all whites just came in."

"Bet."

Tress was his eyes and ears in the KL. Always had been and always would be. Afta' gettin off one last quick li'l round until lata, AB got dressed and made his way to the hood. The commute was only a good ten minutes away. Fifteen during traffic, so it took him no time to pull up on his cousin.

"Ari got yo' ass locked all up in the crib and shit for days, my nigga. Where they do that at?"

Audric chuckled as he hopped inside of Tress' Charger. They always smoked a blunt before they went to re-up for the week.

"Nigga, yo' ass been laid up way befo' me. Surprised you and Manda ain't married yet, wit' yo' sprung ass."

"Shit, man. We close. Shorty ain't goin' nowhere, and I ain't lettin' 'er, you feel me."

"On God. Shit been a'ight these ways?"

"Cool as a mu'fuckin' fan, yo'. Ain't shit been crackin' since we smoked Runo. Them niggas ain't really want it."

TAUGJAYE

That's that shit that AB loved to hear. They murked Runo's ass right before the new year rolled ova'. Audric wasn't goin' into '09 wit' that beef lingerin' on. It was Runo who offed Dutch when it all boiled down. He admitted to it just moments before AB emptied out a clip into his dome. Jealous ass niggas could neva' make it far in this lifetime. Nigga not only was tryna take they crew out, but he was all in his feelin's when he saw Dutch leavin' Leah's crib one day. He'd always wanted Leah, but shorty neva' gave him no play. It was just enough to tip the scale and push him to pull a trigga.

Audric was still fucked up ova' that shit. His boy basically lost his life ova' some pussy, 'cause Runo shoulda' known that takin' AB out so he could have his spot wasn't neva' gon' happen. King ain't fuck wit' them snoops like that in the first place, so that shit was short lived.

Just the thought of Dutch made AB reach for the 5th of Hen that was on the floor by his feet. He poured up for his nigga and took a long gulp to the head. His cousin did too. They was missin' the fuck outta they potna. Shit wasn't the same wit' out him, but they knew he was restin' well.

A Black Dodge Durango came creepin' up the street behind them wit' it's lights off. Audric and Tress were so deep into the lyrics from Lil' Wayne's "I Miss My Dawgs" playin' through the speaker system that, it was too late when bullets started ringin'. It sounded like an army was on the block wit' the way nun' but choppas fired in the air. The rounds were so powerful that it caused Tress' ride to rock back and forth until their clips emptied.

After the police was called and they made it to the crime scene, Tress was found wit' seven holes in his head, and Audric was slumped ova' the dash wit' bullets riddled throughout his entire upper body.

***

1 WEEK LATER

The bass from the party speakers wasn't loud enough. She couldn't get high enough. Ari knew she had no business smokin' anyway, but truth be told, that was the least of her worries right now. Ery'body on 14th street was lit in celebration of AB and Tress' homecoming that afternoon, succeeding the burial.

She tried her best to get into the groove of the jam session. The block was filled from one end to the otha' wit' niggas from all ova' St. Louis City and Counties, payin' they respects. Ery'body was rockin' Crip-blue R.I.P. shirts wit' both they faces on it. Some wore shirts that had Dutch's face added to the duo, too. The city had lost three urban legends wit' no names behind the madness.

Ari was just kissin' his lips. Audric had just told her that he loved her, then God had to take him away from her. Just when life was remainin' steady. She didn't understand it. Didn't wanna understand it. Manda was torn to pieces behind Tress' death too. They just found out that she was three months pregnant and was lookin' forward to raisin' they baby, but Ari was takin' both of they deaths harder than anyone.

Harder than they crew was.

Harder than Auntie Angie.

She grew up wit' Tress.

Knew that nigga since she was eleven and rough lookin'. That was her mu'fuckin brotha. When ery'body else in this world turned they backs on her, he didn't. Tress pushed her to look forward to betta' days, and now, she had to spend those same days wit' out him *and* the man she grew to truly love.

Tears fell down her cheeks as she hid behind her Dior shades.

Numb wasn't even the word.

And neitha' was hurt.

There'd foreva' be a hole in her heart that was now three times as bigger. The three closest people to her had been cropped, cut out, and eliminated from the picture. If it wasn't for Manda, Ari probably woulda' sliced her left wrist complete the fuck off. Who knows what would've happened had she not busted in the room and took the blade from her.

Her soul was cryn'.

Her spirit was broken. Had she not come face-to-face wit' a positive pregnancy test just this mornin' herself, shorty woulda' blew her brains out wit' the Glock that Audric kept stashed in the nightstand.

Her bottom lip trembled when Manda walked up to her. She threw her arms around Ari's neck. Ari wrapped her arms around Manda's waist, and they cried on each otha's shoulda; in front of ery'body. This shit was a nightmare. A nightmare that they both was so desperately beggin' to be woken up from, but...this was real life, and they couldn't just focus on themselves anymore. They had li'l legends to raise in absence of they daddies. The Bowden family tree had to continue.

"Ari."

The voice shocked them so much that both Ari and Manda turned around. She knew that voice from anywhere. And lo and behold, there stood Leah wit' tears streamin' down her face. Her six month belly could be seen behind her grey, puffy, Roc-A-Wear coat wit' the furry hood. No matta' what the weather was, the hood wouldn't let the day go by wit' out showin' AB and Tress some love.

Ari didn't know how to feel. A part of her was ecstatic to see Leah after so long, but anotha' part of her knew she was only doin' this for Tress. Not because she truly wanted to. Or, so she thought.

"I'm not here just because of Tress," Leah started wit' tears that continued to profusely run down her eyes. "I won't even lie though, Ari. Tress pulled up on me a coupla' days before the shootin', checkin' up on the baby. And while he was thur', he checked me real muthafuckin' good for allowing shit to go this far.

I've been wantin' to talk to you for a while now. Especially after I found out that my momma was shootin' up heroin, and that's why she'd been actin' crazy. She'd been doin' it for like, a month before y'all's fight. I was scared of what she might do if she found out I tried to talk to you, and

I'm sorry. I'm so mu'fuckin' sorry, Ari. Fat Momma's daddy took her from my momma—who, I haven't seen in two weeks now."

"Leah," Ari started wit' a cracked voice. "I don't need yo' sympathy."

"It's not sympathy, Ari. It's the truth. I put that on ery'thing I love. Ari, I put this on Fat Momma and my baby. I'm doin' this because I want to. I miss you, too. So fuckin' much, friend. I'm so fucked up behind Tress being killed, and I know how you feel losin' a nigga that you loved. You was there for me when Dutch was killed, and I'm hur' for you. Best friend, if that's how you still see me…I'm so fuckin' sorry. Please believe me. Please forgive me, even though you have ery' right not to afta' the way I treated you."

Manda stood thur' wit' tears runnin' down her cheeks as well, waitin' on her girl to respond. She knew Ari still loved and missed Leah, too. They always talked about it. So she was proud of them for lettin' bygones be bygones when they pulled each other in for an overdue hug.

Ari ain't have no more fight left in her. Somethin' just had to give, and if makin' up wit' her friend was gon' help lighten this load, then that's what she'd do.

The block didn't start to clear out until well afta' one in the mornin'. They woulda' partied until the sun rose if it wasn't for the temperature droppin' down to the low thirties. Ari, Manda, and Leah was all preparin' to leave until Crackhead Don had stopped them. He needed to have a li'l word wit' Ari before he dipped and shook the Lou. He knew he'd be wanted after lettin her in on the info that couldn't be held back from her.

***

King Pharaoh was down in the basement countin' ova' his weekly profits. It made him feel a way starin' at the extra eighty grand he normally wouldn't see when Audric and Tress was livin'. Not givin' a fuck about messin' up his plush carpet, he poured out some of his Moét for two of the three best niggas he'd eva' had on his team. Shit was surreal, but afta' all these years of bein' in the game, it was sumn' he'd grown to accept: ery'body couldn't always go to the next level wit' you.

That was code.

It was his last night bein' on 14th street. Afta' his soldiers were murked, it was time that he closed up shop and relocated to a safer location where niggas couldn't clock they moves. The KL was startin' to get too hot, and that shit was bad for business.

He was nose deep into sniffin' up his third line of coke. King was so focused on his next high that he ain't notice the shadow to the left of him creepin' down the stairs. Just as he sat up and wiped his nose free from the residue, a bullet pierced his chest, and a second one blew a hole in his head.

Ari felt her shouldas relax as she watched the smoke emit from the silencer that was attached to her Glock. King Pharaoh's blood leaked onto the sofa as tears cascaded down her face.

The same nigga that AB and Tress rode for…

TAUGJAYE

I mean, straight respected, and protected...had put the hit out on them. She hadn't been able to sleep ery' since Crackhead Don told her that shit.

Audric mighta' been gone, but the shit he left behind wasn't. He'd taught her ery'thing he fuckin' knew and learned, and now, Ari had to take that same information and survive in this cold ass world wit' out him...as the new plug.

To Be Continued

Author TaugJaye's Catalog

Standalones
*MONSTROSITY
(Formerly known as Love From A Boss)
*Boo'd Up With A St. Louis Goon
*Heart Up For Ransom
*Boss Bitches Need Love, Too
*Sweet In The Middle
*Do it For the Kulture: Love in the Lou
*All These Kisses: Love From A Young Thug
*Falling For A Young Baller
*Your Love Keeps Pulling Me Back
(Full version coming soon)

Series
*Sweet Like Rosé 1-2
*Power of the P: Love, Sex, & Thugs 1-2
Lover's Until the Grave 1-3
* Behind Closed Doors
*New Year, New Drama: A LaCroix Holiday
(Part 2 of BCD)
*Rich Sex 1-2
*Give Me A Project Chick: ARI
*Memoirs of A Bad Bitch
(Part 2 of ARI coming soon)

Novellas/Novelettes
*Christmas With My Westside Hitta
*Diggin' On You
*Down To My Last Breath
*New Year, New Bae, New ME

Conncect with Me!

Facebook:
TaugJaye
Author TaugJaye
Ink Mobb (Beyond the Ink…)

Instagram:
Taugjaye
Author TaugJaye

Made in the USA
Middletown, DE
24 October 2020